NIGHT WATCH

Also by Jon May

Divers - From Piper Alpha To The Gulf War
Salvage - From the South China Sea to the Caribbean Coast
Smoke On The Water

NIGHT WATCH

JON MAY

A DEEP SEA STORY

First published in paperback in 2019
by Sixth Element Publishing
on behalf of Jon May

Sixth Element Publishing
Arthur Robinson House
13-14 The Green
Billingham TS23 1EU
Tel: 01642 360253
www.6epublishing.net

ISBN 978-1-912218-77-6

British Library Cataloguing in Publication Data. A catalogue record for this book is available from the British Library.

Printed in Great Britain.

This is the story of one ship, her crew, and a wreck. Some of the details are fiction, but all of the events are based on real ships, real events and real people.

As long as human beings have ventured onto the sea, as long as there have been ships, ships have wrecked. The results are nearly always a human tragedy, in the final analysis, as a long-standing medical colleague once said, "You can't breathe water." Sometimes, the stress of the wreck, and the need to survive, brings out the best in humanity. Sometimes it brings out the worst. In the end, no matter how we moralise and pass judgement, the sea is neutral and will always be so.

JM 2019

CHAPTER ONE

The tropical evening was humid, with the temperature hovering around eighty degrees. It felt as if you could take a double handful of the air and wring the water out of it in little streams.

Alongside the rickety old passenger wharf in Miri, in rural Malaysia, the inter-island ferry San Fong was waiting for the last of her cargo of migrant labourers to embark. They were the usual mix of itinerant agricultural workers heading for other islands, following the endless cycle of crops, with a scattering of neatly dressed businessmen in grey sarongs and white shirts, carrying briefcases as a badge of their superior status.

Scattered among them was the general stream of migratory humanity that endlessly wanders the islands looking for work. Some were searching for education, some for wealth, some were simply following a distant dream of a better life, that always receded like a mirage as they approached it. In other words, the passengers were a fairly average Thursday night crop of clients, to be checked aboard and stowed below, or perhaps, for the few that could afford it, ushered to a tiny, far from luxurious cabin below decks.

Few of them could run to the expense of a cabin. The rest of the passengers, by far the majority, crammed themselves into the open spaces down below, marking out a territory on a clear space of carpeted companionway, rolling out sleeping bags, or even just blankets, to spend the night.

On the wharf, food sellers fried spicy delicacies in sooty woks over charcoal fires, and hawked their wares to the passing trade. The passengers who were left on deck, those who could find nothing more luxurious in the way of accommodation, staked themselves out a bit of open space to sling a hammock, or lay a thin padded mattress on the warm plating under the open sky.

There was a hierarchy even among the passengers left on the open deck. Those who knew best picked the choice spots, well away from the main trafficked areas, and well clear of the funnel, where the ocean breezes would ground the stinking plume of her exhaust. They stayed well away from the ventilator stacks too, for directly below those stacks were the places where a blast of warm air, drawn from below, would turn tropical warmth into blistering discomfort during the night.

On the bridge, Andy Fitzroy, was going through the routine of preparing for sea. He was, he would have been the first to agree, too old for the rough trade of the inter-island ferries, but then again, after fifty years at sea, he was too old to be doing anything much else. The sea was all he knew, the only life he could remember with any clarity, and the Indonesian Ferries, with their total lack of regulation and their willingness to overlook certain gaps in the certification of their deck officers, were the best berths he was likely to get. Andy was, at least in his mind, old navy. Like many men after a long career at sea he looked not so much marked by a lifetime on salt water as actually a part of the ocean itself, as much at home on water as a seabird. His tan was deep mahogany and his vivid blue eyes were two chips of icy colour in a tangle of brown wrinkles. Andy was old time merchant fleet and proud of it.

The San Fong was nearly as old as he was, but, unlike a good many of the old rust buckets that sail between the islands, she had been built as a ferry – albeit for a very different run. The ship had started life as the Lady of the Isles, far to the North, running out of Mallaig on the West Coast of Scotland, and she had gradually, as age and dereliction overtook her, been passed down the chain of efficiency, always moving into less regulated regimes, finally ending in the South China Sea.

Andy, from his prominent viewpoint on the bridge, looked down at the heaving mass of humanity on the foredeck with distaste.

"Mr Cheung," he said to his number two, "try to get the buggers to leave a clear walkway, will you? At this rate we'll never get to the capstan to slip the bloody moorings."

Cheung, the Cantonese deck officer, pulled a face. "Wei," he said.

In many ways, Cheung Chao was Andy's polar opposite, son of a fishing family who had become a sailor almost because it seemed to be his birthright, he was merchant fleet through and through. Those two constantly bickered at a low level like an old married couple.

Andy, even after all those years, was still a stickler for naval protocol. "No, no," he said. "You don't say 'Wei' to me, Mr Cheung. We may be on a fucked up old inter island ferry but we will still have some seamanship on this bridge, Mister. You call me Mr Fitzroy, or Captain."

Cheung pulled a face. "Wei," he said.

"What?" said Andy, rising to the bait, in spite of himself.

"Wei," said Cheung deliberately. "Wei. Wei. Wei. You don't like, you get another fucking deck officer."

It is the experience of rank that marks out a good captain. Andy refused to rise to the bait. Instead of arguing, he said, "Just shift those bloody passengers, will you, Mister? We are due under way in five minutes. I've no wish to miss the bloody tide."

Twenty minutes later, in a cloud of dirty diesel smoke, with much flurrying of her propellers, and a nasty rumble from the prop shaft bearings, the San Fong edged away from the jetty, and pulled past the old Chinese graveyard on the riverbank, heading for the sandbar, and the open sea. There were no fanfares, no ceremony about her departure, even though, after so many years' service, it was to be her very last voyage. The graves of the ancestors, looking for all the world like tiled primrose coloured double beds set into the earth, looked down on the passing traffic impassively, as befits the last resting place of good, deceased, Taoists.

Five hundred miles to the south, in an anonymous patch of open ocean, Met buoy 4/556720.SCS was busying about its robotic activities. Just as the San Fong cleared the dock, and started out to sea, the buoy recorded an odd set of circumstances.

The first oddity was a drop in barometric pressure. There was nothing strange in that, not in itself, but open water pressure changes are usually small and gradual, and this one was large and very, very, rapid. At the same moment the air temperature began to rise, and surface wind speed showed a sudden shift. What had been a light breeze stiffened to a sharp breath of air that ruffled the empty ocean. Out in the empty spaces, where few ships plied their trade, a weather system was, almost unnoticed, beginning to gather strength.

Anonymity is a tough act to maintain, even in the more isolated parts of the world. At the area Met Centre, an automated system considered the figures relayed by the buoy for an age of computer time. It compared previous occasions in its memory banks, searching for a similar situation, and considered the results. Five seconds later the system made a decision. It began to broadcast an automated 'be aware' warning to shipping. The 'heads up' went out on the international maritime met frequency. Typhoon Betsy, the second of the season was gestating, ready to be born.

CHAPTER TWO

Far to the south, Salvage Vessel DSV Typhoon Star was on her way to a scheduled towing job. As the weather grew steadily worse, the 'heads up' typhoon warning from the area Met triggered the start of a lockdown. All over the ship, watertight doors were closed and dogged tightly shut. Those of her crew who were normally employed on deck, took refuge where they could. With the ship battened down against the weather, no more open deck work, other than the bare essentials of sailing the ship, would be done. The long wait for the storm to blow itself out had begun.

At such times, when crewmen gather with idle time to spare, craic sessions begin. In earlier centuries, in the days of sail, there was a belief, mainly among ship's officers, that such times were dangerous. Crews were often only loosely held together by harsh naval discipline, and free time was a chance for long suppressed grievances, over poor food, perhaps, or unpopular officers, or maybe just the lack of prize money, to boil over into open insurrection.

On the more positive side, sailors have always told stories. Many of the stories told in a thousand dockside bars are distortions, or at least embroideries of the truth. They are tales, coloured by the need to impress, to demonstrate the sailors' superiority to landsmen, or even to persuade gullible listeners to spring for another drink.

Cut from another bolt of cloth altogether are the stories that sailors tell to each other. These stories are lifelines that run through the industry. They are an informal information network, less vital than in former times, when word of mouth was the main news medium, but still there, an undercurrent running below the modern ebb and flow of work.

Informal or not, no longer vital or not, the truth is, that, at sea, odd things really do happen, no less today than in the days of sail. Of course today there are fewer real mysteries. After all, a single survivor from a disaster is enough to destroy the mystique of a loss at sea, and to turn a latter day 'Mary Celeste' back into a simple industrial accident.

Yet the strange and the unexpected happens still. The two thirds of the planet that are covered by salt water are still an unexplored zone in many respects. Above all, the human factor, the infinitely variable mix of personalities that make up a crew, isolated as they are on the small island community of a ship surrounded by an alien medium, will perhaps always be an unexplored country, with its own unfathomable rules.

On that night, with a tropical storm already blowing, a full typhoon coming, and the ship fighting through violent crossing seas, Typhoon Star's crew looked for sheltered areas to escape the open spaces on deck.

Often, at such a time, one especially favoured shelter is the almost womb-like atmosphere of the diving control room. There, the constant temperature, maintained by the steady whisper of the AC system, the subdued lighting, and the comfortable seating (not a frivolous luxury, but needed to allow twelve hour watches observing the instrumentation), offers a refuge. It is a place where one can ignore the realities of the storm outside for a while.

Typhoon Betsy was the second of her ilk that year, and she was a monster, with wind speeds of over a hundred and fifty knots in gusts. Around the eye of the storm, violent crossing seas gave the self-steering system a constant challenge to hold her head to the wind and weather.

As luck would have it, the storm had caught the Star on the way to a job. A simple tow, which they had not yet taken up, was turning into a marathon, before the job had even rightly begun. Of course it could have been worse, far worse, if the storm had blown up twenty hours later. Lugging a deadweight of fifteen thousand tonnes at the end of a hundred metre long bridle through such seas would have turned a tough break into a living nightmare.

Typhoon Star was built, as they say, 'to take it'. She was structured like a deep-sea tug. She was massively over-engined, and strong enough in the bows to break ice at need. Faced with heavy weather, she simply rode the seas like a stubborn cork.

For three weeks prior to that job, the Star had been alongside, tied up in port waiting for work. Her crew had been occupied, in the way of idle sailors, with taking in the dubious delights of the few dockside bars.

They stood standby watches, endlessly maintaining systems that required no further maintenance, idling on minimal pay, and waited for the call to action. Waited in fact for a series of blasts on the ship's whistle to call them from wherever they happened to be. That much was tradition in the salvage business, even in the age of electronic communications. The waiting had gone on for weeks until, out of the blue, the long awaited contract came in, not as often happens, via the radio room, but via a telex message from head office in Amsterdam… and it was literally a telex. Antiquated though it might be in these days of electronics, telex was still used to foil eavesdropping by the competition.

From the start it seemed straightforward. A freighter had broken down, and was now partially disabled out in the open ocean. The casualty was in no immediate danger. According to the telex, all she needed was a simple tow to a repair yard. It was the maritime equivalent of a breakdown tow to the local garage.

In most, more regulated areas of the world, it could have been no more dramatic than that.

A simple radio call, and a basic legal agreement between owners and salvage company, is normally something that can be arranged with a friendly exchange of emails. Recovery of a broken down vessel is the routine business of the oceans. In the UK there was, until recently, even a government sponsored fleet of coastguard tugs waiting, strategically placed around the coast, to recover casualties.

The Far East is not the UK. Salvage here is an almost piratical enterprise, crewed very often by sailors who would have been happy in the golden years of the eighteenth century buccaneers. They are men, born out of their time, who find the regulated, ordered world of the twenty-first century chafes on their world view. To those who find the frontier spirit an embarrassment, or an anachronism, this attitude and mindset can seem almost a danger to the order of things. To others these men are heroic. Neither judgement is the entire truth. They are sailors, and to real seafarers there is no need to apply a more analytic description that that.

CHAPTER THREE

Out on the fringes of the storm, the crew of the San Fong were beginning to notice the effects of the weather. It was getting on for full dark but the turbulence was breaking the surface of the sea and throwing constant flickers of pale blue green light from the phosphorescence.

As the wind speed picked up, edging towards the lower limits of a gale, the first white flecks of broken water were starting to show up. From his viewpoint on the bridge, Andy Fitzroy regarded the ocean with some distaste. Those first white horses had long signalled far worse to come.

Like many of the vessels in that sector, San Fong had no automated Met reporting system, relying instead on the informal radio network of ships in the immediate area to keep track of the shifts in the weather. The automated 'heads up' had passed her by, but, in truth, Andy relied on an older, far more visceral, system of tracking the weather than electronics.

Over the years, his experience of what the sea could do had been tuned to an exquisite degree, and, that night, he fully expected rough weather. By ten o'clock the deck passengers were already deserting the open spaces on deck as they huddled in clots in the corridors, and, at the first suggestion of movement, corkscrewing the old ship as she moved through the water, Andy took over the bridge watch himself, and began the long routine of balancing the throttles and the rudder against the changing run of the seas.

Looking out at the water through the old fashioned spinning disc of the clear screen, he took a swig from a bottle of local hooch and mentally set his shoulders against the elements. The San Fong was already in the cyclonic turbulence that whipped around the eye of the typhoon, and her crew were all too aware of what such a storm might do. The weather was already bad, and, they knew, had the potential to go towards the catastrophic.

In such circumstances, there was little hope of making useful progress against the weather. For now the only way was to hold her head to the seas and wait the battering out, until the wind abated. Down below decks, passengers and crew alike listened apprehensively to the increasing turmoil, as the inclinometer on the panel below the bridge windows swayed wildly.

The inclinometer is one of the oldest of navigational tools. It is no more than a weight on a pivot that blindly follows the pull of gravity to drive a pointer on a scale that runs from vertical (meaning dead calm) to a swing of fifty degrees or so. At the far end of the scale some long ago comedian had taped an alternative, less formal, set of measurements. At the end, at the extreme limit of movement, that would indicate a roll of fifty degrees and more, it said, in English, 'Oh shit' in neat red letters. As the movement increased, the inclinometer scale became, for the first time in years, an object of interest on the bridge.

CHAPTER FOUR

Typhoon Star had no inclinometer in dive control, there was no need of one, but the little room had the disconcerting effect of feeling like a washing machine drum on spin cycle. The crew, all professional seafarers, were well accustomed to violent movement. The sudden shifts of gravity hardly raised a comment.

Taff Jennings was nominally a leading hand, though he was actually a master mariner with the experience of decades behind him. He lit a fresh pipe of pungent tobacco, and, after it was burning to his satisfaction, he joined in the conversation in the dive control room.

Taff Jennings was as Welsh as his name. A small man as round as he was tall, and dark skinned and swarthy like many of the Northern Welsh. He was always dreaming of the valleys. Always intending to find that one last big job that would clear him enough to buy a bit of mountain pasture and raise sheep. In this fantasy he saw himself on winter evenings, sitting in front of an open wood fire, maybe dreaming of the time when his horizon had been the place where the sea met the sky, and his home was as wide as the whole ocean. Always intending to go home, he somehow never quite raised that elusive last few thousand that would have crystallised the dream.

There was always something that got in the way. Often it was a sure-fire salvage job that didn't quite pay off. Once it was a partnership in a bar in an exotic distant port. Twice, the dream failed because of a woman. One by one they seemed to let Taff down, but through it all, he remained a gentle soul, strange though that was for a man who listed a stretch in Special Forces among his working credits.

For Taff, at least, the dream never quite faded. It was always a bright mirage that forever drew him on towards a destination that he never quite reached. He had a quiet voice that still carried through the fug of the control room, and the racket that penetrated from the gathering storm outside. There was still music in that accent, a ghost of those long ago valleys, where he had grown to manhood and a life at sea, far from the rolling hills of home.

"It was maybe ten years back," he said. "I don't rightly remember the year, but I had been working the old Dubai Moon as mate. We were officially a tug/supply ship but really we were running drinks up the Gulf from Dubai to the dry states further north. I'd had a good run, we'd been working that game for a good eighteen months, making good money too, then came word that the religious police in Saudi were putting together enough evidence to slap us down on the next trip. I'd no wish to see the inside of a Saudi jail, so I scraped together enough cash to get the hell out of there. Then I met this man. Well, you know how it is, boys, he said he'd just done a stretch fishing on the Grand Banks, and that the money there was unbelievable. Course that sounded good to me, so I bought a one way ticket to Alaska, filed a seafarer's visa, and left the Gulf behind. Good job too it was, the buggers busted the rest of the crew six weeks afterwards, three years they got, every man jack of them. Well, if any of you have ever worked that Grand Banks fishery you will know how it works. On the dockside in Dutch Harbour, there's this office, well it's really a wooden shack you know? Like most buildings in Dutch. So I went in, showed my seaman's tickets and asked if there was any hope of a berth, you see, and after the usual humming and haa-ing the man behind the counter said here was one boat that was due to sail that night, and she was short of a deckhand. He said she was called the 'Ellen G' which meant nothing to me, not right then, and if I wanted to give her a try, she was alongside the dock, and I'd to go and talk to the skipper – a laddo called Jimmy Bowen…"

Taff – leading hand

Those crab boats are something else, boys, none of them much over eight hundred tonne, and looking like an old coaster with a big stack of iron cages on the forward deck and a bit of hydraulic gear to handle the pots.

The skipper was right there, on the bridge, and he was a big Yankee with a dead slow southern accent. Took him an hour to say anything, if you see what I mean. Well, we talked a few minutes about what I'd done before that, what sea time I had, and so on, and, after that, he was ready to chance me as a deckhand/greenhorn.

"Well, then," he said. "Thing is, Taff – you know, that's kind of a strange name to my hearing – there's not much to this job, so long as you're a seaman. It's just mainly baiting the pots, and swinging 'em over the side, and then hauling the string when the work's done and dropping the crab into the tanks below decks. With your sea time, you'all should have no problems with the deck work. Only thing is, you need to watch the hoist. Those pots weigh near on a tonne, and you don't want to try to stop one with your head, you understand? Okay, take yourself down to meet the others. George, the deck boss, is a pretty good old boy, the rest are local Aleuts, you understand?"

I said I did.

And he said, after a moment's thought, "Okay, just one thing. You'all hear we got ourselves a bad rep this season? No? Well, that useless piece of shit in the seaman's office should have said. I don't want no one getting the gee-gaws like a girl at her first sight of a man thing, not out there in the Goddam Bering Sea. So you best hear this from me. We had ourselves a few accidents. Well I'm saying a few – we lost three men this season – all of 'em just vanished in the night, over the side, I guess, there ain't no place else to go out there. It ain't exactly unusual. Most seasons, a boat maybe loses a man, but this run of luck, well, people are getting to think the Ellen G ain't a lucky boat, puts a lot of people right off. Just thought you should know before you'all sign articles. You understand?"

"I think so," I said. "I don't believe in unlucky boats."

I remember he looked at me very directly like, as if he was summing things up and making sure if I would do, like.

Then he said, "Okay, Taff isn't it? Well, Taff, you got yourself a job. We sail at midnight, so, if you want to spend a little time getting to know the ladies of Dutch Harbour, now's the time. Otherwise I'll get George to show you your bunk and you can settle in."

Three hours later or so I met the rest of the crew. They were Aleuts like he said. Local labour, you know? Working out of the Aleutian Islands. Little blokes, you see, but still they were good sailors, and over the first three days as we steamed out into the Bering Sea, they taught me how to run the gear. There's not much to it, you see? Just a tilt table to drop the pots over the side and a friction winch to haul them back in afterwards. All of it is basic stuff.

After three days we started to drop the pots and there were the usual hitches. It looks like nothing, you see, swinging a crab pot, but they're big, and heavy too, and, once that pot hits the water, it's going to the bottom no matter what. So you've to watch the tethers as they feed out, 'cause if one gets around your leg as it goes out, well, you go with it, boyo, and there's no saving you. Mind, those Aleut guys were bloody marvels at the job and I hardly met the number two 'til we started to pull the string a day or so after.

So… what to tell you about Jimmy Brown, boys? Well, he

was a big bugger, wide over the shoulders like, and he was real pale, his hair very near white, his eyebrows too, so I guess it was natural, not bleached, and he had these strange hands, soft, you know? Like a man who never handles steel, or rope neither. Oh, and he had this tattoo. Well, nothing funny in that boys, but it was one I'd never seen before. Well, I thought I'd seen it all in tats, I worked with a guy once had a red duster right over the width of his arse, and an anchor on his dick too, on the *inside* of his foreskin it was, and that must have stung something rotten, but this was some kind of symbol thing. Later on, after it was all over, I found it was the mark of the White Aryan Brotherhood, some racist mob in the States. Well, right then I could make nothing of it – wouldn't have mattered if I had, I reckon, enough of those yanks have street gang tats from when they are growing up. It means bugger all… 'cept in his case, well… We were doing good, see, tanks three parts full with Opillio crab and the crew looking to spend their money before we'd even landed them.

Then it happened. I remember that night so well. It was as cold as a witch's tit on deck, bloody sea ice forming all around us in those patches that look like oil on the surface, and still no let up in the work, see. Jake, one of the Aleut crew, was headed down into the engine room 'cause of some problem or other. It was nothing big, just an electrical breaker that kept tripping out, and stopping the pump for the hydraulics, but it was a pain, 'cause it was slowing down the hauling and you never knew when it would suddenly go out altogether. Anyhow Jake is half way down the ladder to the switchgear when he hears a weird noise. Afterwards he said it was like a dog growling, see. At first he thought it was some bit of gear running rough, well, you all know the sort of funny noises that you get in the engine room. Then he gets a good look.

Well, he gets to bottom of the engine room ladder and there it all was, Freddy, one of the other deckhands, was lying on the checker plate by number two diesel, his head was right up against the sump, and there was blood all around him in a pool. Well, that was bad, but worse than that, Jimmy Brown was kneeling there beside him and he was lapping the blood like a fucking dog drinking from a bowl.

There was blood all down his chin and Jake said he raised his head and sort of grinned at him. Next second Jimmy was on his feet and coming at him and screaming all sorts of crazy stuff. Well, you have to give Jake credit for speed, lads. There was this pegboard next to the stairway, and there were ready use tools racked up there on the bulkhead. Jake, he whipped off a shifter spanner from the rack, a big one it was by all accounts, and he whacked Jimmy across the head as hard as he could.

Now that mad bugger was big, but he goes down like a sack of spuds and Jake starts yelling blue bloody murder for someone to help him. Next day we're on our way back to Dutch, and Jimmy is tied up on a bunk like a turkey on Christmas Eve. Well, when we get to Dutch Harbour the sheriff is waiting there with about twenty armed men. Never knew they had so many police in Dutch. You'd think we had Bin Laden aboard. Anyhow, they took Jimmy off. I never saw him after that, see, but I heard all about it.

They locked him up right away, not fit to stand trial of course, as mad as a bloody toilet he was, boys. Thing was, aside from that one deckhand he'd attacked, there was never any proof that he'd had anything to do with the other guys who went missing, but he did kill two other patients in the place where they held him, before he died himself. Now I'm not a superstitious man, boys, but I hope they buried that bugger with a stake through his heart.

CHAPTER FIVE

And, with that final pronouncement, Taff settled back in his seat and sucked on his pipe contentedly. In the near dark there was only a dim shape and the coal of his pipe bowl glowing and pulsing in the dark as he drew on it.

Unsurprisingly, after that story, there were a few minutes of silence as the men thought about it. Finally Zac, the medic, broke the mood.

Zac Rasmussen was one of those metabolic oddities who seemed to eat non-stop and yet never gained an ounce of weight. He was good at his job, if a little cold. They said of him, among the crew, that he was a technician above everything else, good at repairing the sick and injured, but not a man to go to expecting sympathy. A ship's medic from his days in the Royal Navy, if Zac had a fault, it was that of only seeing good in his crew mates. He rarely disagreed with anyone, and had never, to anyone's recall, ever had an argument that lasted beyond a day or so. He was a peaceful man, a gentleman in all sense of the word. You might have expected that he could have been bullied, but there was about him that air of a Sicilian 'man of respect', that went far beyond that glacial exterior.

Surrounding him, like an invisible cloak, there was an air of invincibility, a sense that, although he never openly resorted to force to settle his point of view on others, if ever he were forced to the point, the result would have been catastrophic. Because of that air of invulnerability, he remained a peaceful, easy going man who everyone respected and trusted rather than liked. No one, as far as anyone was aware, had ever been on a run ashore with Zac Rasmussen. Like many Scandinavians he had a precision of language and a crispness of diction that sometimes sounded strange among the league of nations mix, and casual profanity of the rest of the team. So, when he spoke up from the blood red shadows, everyone automatically listened.

Zac waited until he was sure that they were all paying attention. After a few moments, the only sounds were the thump and hiss of the waves against the hull, and the small sucking sound as Taff drew on his pipe. Finally when he was sure of his audience, Zac began his story.

"Strange things happen," he said. "And, well, madmen will always do strange things. But it is not only the insane who are a risk to the rest of the crew. Sometimes people act for what they think is the best, and things still go wrong for no one's fault that you can see. In Norway, we have a saying that if the Gods have decided to torment you there is no help for it. There was this one time, a few years ago it was, I don't exactly remember the year but it was a while back…"

Zac – the medic

I never had any real religion, you know. Back home in the mountains they all went to this little wooden church, my dad, my mother, all my family. I was taken there whether I wanted, or not. But by the time I was fifteen I had made up my mind that it was all crap. I looked at this old protestant minister with his red face and white hair, standing up there in the pulpit telling them all about how good God was and how Jesus had saved their souls, and I thought, this is fucking fairy stories, good for old women

18

and small kids. They used to tell stories about the mountains, about the trolls and what not, about the king of the mountains who kept his court up in the high country. I couldn't make it feel any different to the bloody stories from the bible. It was just the same thing, old shit written down instead of just old people talking.

So I joined the navy. First the Norwegian military, then the merchant fleet, and all the time I got by without giving a shit about religion, and not believing in all that crap about ghosts and shapeshifters and blood drinkers. I reckon, you see, it was all the same old shit. I worked every day saving lives, and I learned a thousand things that could go wrong with the human body, but all that time I never once saw a soul.

Well, it was one winter a few years back, I was working one of the Seaways boats not far from home. We were up in the north eastern sector of the North Sea. We were scanning a line, just following a pig that was running from Oseburg platform to the beach inspecting the pipeline. You all know how fucking boring that can be. Mile after mile following the signal from that bloody radio transmitter and looking at the information it sent back.

Well, late one night we get this signal, yes? It was bloody big, whatever it was, big enough to worry the bosses and get us into a full survey mode. We noted the spot, just a bit of empty ocean to look at it, and carried on with following the pig until we got to the Zeepipe junction, where our pipe joined the main matrix, and we could break off chasing the pig and go back to looking for that big signal.

By the time we get to do a full ROV survey on the thing it was well into winter. It was cold that night, even for the northern fields, and there were odd bits of brash ice floating by. Anyway we put the camera down to take a look at the bottom and, well, we could hardly miss that wreck.

Now we need to go back a way. By the second year of World War Two the U-boat fleet was knocking all kinds of shit out of passing shipping, but by 1944 most of the menace was done with. The allies had developed sonar, so the U-boats could not hide so well, and they had radar to track them on the surface. By the year's end, the U-boat aces who had sailed back to their bases with the pennants flying to show how many ships they had sunk, went down in their turn. Quite a few were lost without trace.

That wreck was the remains of one of those missing boats. The ROV swam over it and photographed it, and bit by bit, we got a picture of the wreck. She was lying a bit on one side in the mud on the bottom, and she was sealed up like she was still ready for sea. We could still read her pennant number with a bit of careful looking. U733. Later, we found out that she gone missing in 1944 and from that day to this no one knew where she was.

You all know the law on war graves. If a wreck went down with her crew, if that is the last resting place, you treat the ship as a tomb, which I guess in a way it is, and you leave it untouched. As it happened this one was lying well clear of anything that really mattered. It was a few hundred metres clear of the pipeline, so there was no problem. We surveyed the wreck as best we could, noted her exact position for the records, and then… well, that was when it got bloody odd, boys. The first odd thing as far as I can say to my own certain knowledge, was two nights later. I was doing the paperwork in the hospital when I noticed this smell. It was sharp, it stung the back of your nose. Well, at first I thought I'd spilled something. You know in the hospital there are all kinds of chemicals about, but I checked around and there was nothing, and after a bit, I couldn't smell anything so I thought I must have imagined it.

That night, I have this dream for the first time. You are thinking, so what's strange? But the fact is medics have an odd time. You know, in this job, well quite a few guys, they can't take the truth of the job. Yeah, some of them lie wake at night trying to think out how they might have done something different every time they lose a patient. Me, I never do that, you do the job as best you can, no one is ever right all the time. You do what you can and then you live with it. Like they say, take the heat or get the fuck out of the kitchen, yes? But that night I have this dream. In it I was real hot, you know, sweating like, though I never get too hot in my bunk, not even in the tropics. There was this smell like you get in the living chambers after a few weeks under pressure. You know, you life support guys, you try to keep it away, you filter the gas through carbon and Puron, and you clean the filters three times in a week, but still there is this smell of bodies and breath, and old farts. It's not strong but it's there. Every time I treat guys in the chambers I smell that smell as soon as the hatch opens. But in the dream it was dark, nothing except that smell to give away where you are.

And I could think, you know. Most dreams you get carried along in your own head, nothing you can do but watch, like a movie screen. This wasn't like that. I could still think and still move if I wanted to, but it was pitch dark. I've felt like that once before, when I woke up after I spent the night in the system. I'd treated a guy for a busted wrist. It took so long to get it set right I had to stay overnight in the system and do a full decompression through the next day. Anyhow it was that same feeling, waking up and thinking, where the bloody hell am I?

So I just stayed there waiting for my head to catch up with where I was and then there was this smell again, sharp and bitter like a municipal swimming pool in the morning after they get too strong with the disinfectant, yeah?

Right after that I couldn't breathe suddenly, my chest just locked up and the dark starts to come in, coming at me in waves, and I knew. Right then I knew I was dying. So I just lie there and wait for it to be over. There was a few seconds of that and then nothing. After that I woke in my own bunk, just like always, no problem, except a sore arm where I had been lying on it too long.

So it was just a dream, sure, but it sort of carried through to the next day. I couldn't get rid of that feeling of expecting to die. No matter how I try to shake it off, it stays with me. I went through the next day like I was in a trance, you know? We were busy sorting out the formalities of that old sub. Any other wreck we would have just flattened it but we couldn't do that not without special clearance from the beach so we just sat there in the open ocean. 'Standby to standby', you know?

Next off shift I stayed up late watching some old movie. I was not really trying to avoid going to my bunk… but I was, if you understand me, even though I couldn't say it out loud even to myself. When I get to my bunk, I read a book for an hour or so and in the end I go to sleep, and right away I get the dream again. It was the same all over, closed space, dark, that chemical smell and after a few moments there was that fight to breathe.

Well, I know a bit about breakdowns, part of my job, you see, and every now and then some guy on the crew will high side it, so I know what it looks like if a guy starts to lose it, and by then I'm thinking about, maybe it's PTSD. It's the plague of medics, but everything else seemed fine. Sure, I know that you can't diagnose yourself. I try real hard to check myself for symptoms but there's just the dream and for three more nights it came, just the same, four nights in a row.

On the fifth night I took a Valium. I don't like that stuff, it's got too many addicts saying they can't get off it, but I thought, well, if it gets the dream gone, it is worth it, but you see, it didn't. All that Valium did was make it hard to wake up and all the next day I was fogged out. I couldn't trust myself to work, but there was a bit of good luck and it was quiet, as it happened.

The next night was the last on site. We'd done the job as far as we could, mapped the wreck and all that. We were all ready go, but that night the dream came back, and this time there was something else. When I woke up I shifted in my bunk, and I felt a lump in the mattress, like a bit of stuff had got under the sheet somehow? I looked to see what it was, and it was a uniform button. Brass, but it was old and green and corroded. I rubbed it against my hand and the surface crap came off. There was a swastika under it, shiny where I rubbed it.

Now World War Two was a long time ago, but I've read a bit about the Kreigs-Marine and the U-boat service. I recognise that button straight off. It was the same pattern as they used on uniform jackets during the war. I looked at it a bit, wondering, and, after a time, I put it in a specimen jar that sat on my desk.

Right then there was nothing more to be done, so I left it there and went to get breakfast. The boss on that job was Jim Jurgensen. You all know big Jim, lovely guy, but a big talker, you know? Can't shut him up. He loves to talk. Anyhow he sits down in the mess and the next thing he's telling me about the U-boat we'd found that was still just a few hundred metres under our keel.

The German navy reckoned they had worked out what had happened to her. That class of U-boat was only in service for eight months or so. They were built in a rush while the U-boat service was under pressure, and of the fifteen boats they made, eight went down the same way. There was a fault on the ballast control, a design problem, so if it went wrong they got stuck on the bottom.

As for the crew, they had no escape system, poor bastards, either the air would run out, or maybe sea water reached the battery banks in the base of the hull. Later they moved the batteries somewhere safer, but in that class of boat the batteries were lead acid like the ones that start your car. Sea water could sink to the bottom of the pressure hull and reach them. Sea water and battery acid is a bad mix, lads. It makes chlorine gas, you see and it rises up from the deck and you get maybe two breaths before it gets you. Funny stuff chlorine, it attacks everything it touches, dark blue navy uniforms go pale brown, leather rots, and brass buttons go green.

So no sooner had Big Jim done talking and taken himself off to the morning meeting, than I was off back to the hospital. The button was still there on my desk. I took it and I went to the aft deck and stood where the stern roller was right over the sea. I reckon the wreck was right underneath me, so I took that old button and I threw it in. It was a tiny thing, hardly made a splash, then it was gone back to join that old boat and the dreams went along with it.

CHAPTER SIX

Outside, the wind howled its one note idiot song, the ship heaved and pitched as the helmsman fought her back, head to wind, and a few hundred tonnes of water first smashed down on the foredeck and then rushed overboard again through the freeing ports and drained back into the ocean.

"Is it my imagination," asked Fred the El' tech from the shadows, "or is the weather getting worse?"

There was a murmur of agreement around the room

Like just about everyone on the Star, Fred Elman had a long history of seagoing. He had started out with high hopes training first as an engineer in diesel propulsion systems at the Maritime school in Hull, and then serving time on the 'Gin Palaces', as professional sailors scathingly referred to the ocean cruisers.

It was Fred's one weakness that he had a penchant for women. There was no great surprise there, so did very nearly all of the crew, but Fred was attracted to the young and the nubile among the passengers and inevitably when he was found in his own bunk along with the seventeen year old daughter of an American passenger, his contract with the cruise line had been sacrificed to avoid a fuss in the courts. Nor that the girl was unwilling, she was far from it. Nor was the liaison unlawful, at least not by the laws of most countries, but this particular protective daddy had been an American Baptist of the hard shell variety, and the thought of a TV evangelist preaching about the iniquities of the crew of cruise liners was not what the cruise companies PR department was willing to overlook.

Fred went from third engineer with a cushy cabin on C deck of a liner to Electrical Technician on a salvage crew. Still, at least no one gave a damn about who or what he chose to sleep with. Not that there was a lot of scope in that area. Leaving aside the ship's dog, everyone aboard was male and Fred had no inclination towards gay sex. At first he had worked for the independent operators before final joining the salvage crew of a Dutch Salvage operator, finally graduating to senior electrical specialist on the Diving Support Vessel that was the pride of their fleet. With the changing market and the reduced need for saturation diving work, Fred had decided to move to a more secure area of employment, drifting from ship to ship until finally he ended as Senior Electrical Technical Officer on the Star or as they more usually called him, the 'El' tech'.

"Mind you," said Fred, "there's worse things than weather." He stopped for a second until he was sure that the others were listening. "They used to say that worse things happen on the big ships but there was this one time, it involved a sub too, as it happens. It was a bit after Ellie Sorenson took over the job of operation manager at World Wide Ocean Salvage, well, you know how women bosses are in this game, all of them seem to have something to prove…"

Fred – the El' tech

It all started when the boss got the idea of bidding on the contract for the Kursk. None of us were happy with that. After all raising thousands of tonnes of Russian submarine wasn't inside our experience, but then again it wasn't in many other company's experience either. The Yanks did one back in the Cold War, I remember, and they had to build a ship specially to do the job. In the end of course it went to the heavy lift division of Heremac who already had the capacity and the track record to go with it, but Ellie's venture into heavyweight salvage had a spin off that none of us had expected. You all know Ellie Sorenson, that is one crazy lady. Fuck knows what a woman is doing running a salvage tug but there you go. If half the stories they tell about her are true, her daddy did well to leave her the company. Mind you, I have to say she has always been fair to me.

Long, long before they lost the Kursk – back in the closing days of the Cold War it was – another Russian sub had gone a glimmer. She was the ICBM vessel Commosolet or some such name. She were a massive nuclear powered Russian boat that had somehow caught fire and got her pictures all over the news, running on the surface and belching smoke from her conning tower like it were a fucking mill chimney. Anyhow, after a piss poor try at evacuation, she settled to the bottom of the Norwegian Sea. Now it has to be said that among crews who know submarines best – old Lionel was one them, you know? He were an ex-sonar man when he were grey funnel line – they didn't reckon Russian boats.

Anyhow these Russian boats had a reputation with submariners. The reactors that powered them, they were stripped down to the bare minimum of shielding to bring their weight within operational limits, and they gradually irradiated their own crews.

When they finally released the records, long after the event, it showed they were doing rapid crew rotations to give the men a chance of recovery before yet another blast of gamma radiation, and you can bet a pound to a pinch of shit that that were putting the best gloss on it.

Soviet boats were built strong, they were built big, and they were built heavy, but they weren't built safe. Now, exactly what happened to Commosolet before her final dive to the bottom is still argued over. No one knows for sure why the fire, once it had started, was so bloody difficult to contain, but we do know that the seat of the original blaze was back in the stem of the boat near the reactor room.

Well, twenty odd years passed. The wreck was reckoned to be a war grave, 'cause of the poor buggers that she took with her, and she were quietly forgotten. Then there was this routine sampling programme the Noggies set up. It were aimed at following the crap that Sellafield leaked into the North Sea. I reckon they were looking to sue for compensation for the fisheries they had to close off, not that that ever come to anything in end. Anyhow one of their monitors started to pick up scary traces of radiation in the sea water around the wreck site. The levels were low, meaning that, at the worst, there were only tiny quantities of hot material in the water, but they were there and hot material is hot material when all's said and done.

The problem was that there were two possible sources on board that wreck. There was a chance that it was coming from the reactor itself. It were long shut down of course but still with a bloody choice mix of radioactive crap inside it. Well, they thought it might just be leaking. Even Soviet technology were shielded to protect against such a thing but, given the fire, and the fifteen hundred metre dive to the bottom, the shielding might not have been enough. Now that were bad, but maybe there was a second possibility. The hot particles they were finding might just have come from the four forwards torpedo tubes where four nuclear tipped weapons had gone down with the ship. So, twenty years after she sank, it were suddenly important that someone should figure out what was going on down there. The nukes were dangerous in terms of leaks, but a few kilos of leaking plutonium, bad as that might be, would probably get sucked up into the ooze on the bottom and remain locked away there. Course, if it were the reactor core itself that was breaking up, the problem, and the contamination, would be much, much worse. Worst case, if the whole core broke up say, you could write off fisheries in Norwegian waters for a few hundred years, and that would be for starters. After all fish don't hang about on national boundaries, the problem could affect the whole of the bloody North Sea.

Ellie were well chuffed to have landed the job.

"This," she said at the briefing meeting, "will put us on the international map."

I remember thinking that if things went the wrong way it would bloody well do that all right. Anyhow, no one spoke up, though I reckon a few of the lads were thinking that they would pass up being put on the fucking map to avoid this job.

So anyhow she said, "We cannot remain a provincial operation hidden away down here in Asia. It is vital that we move into other areas of influence. Besides, this job is commissioned by the Government of Norway. I don't need to tell you how much diving work they commission."

"There's just one thing about that, boss," someone said. "This job is government owned and financed and that's true. But why did their own company not do the contract? After all Seaways is owned by their Government. This looks like them keeping the responsibility for cock ups at arm's length. Are they just covering their arses in case it all goes pear shaped?"

Now Ellie is a little lady but I don't know anyone who bristles the way she can, boys, especially if she thinks she isn't getting her own way.

"They had no ship available," she said, with what I'm sure she meant to be a disarming smile. To me it looked like the grin on the face of a tiger when it sees its dinner.

For that job we were based and supplied out of Tromso, right on the edge of the Arctic circle. Tromso! There's a place to have a run ashore, boys. First it were seals, then whaling, now it's oil. Still, Tromso! It's sailor town, lads, just the way it always was. See, the sailors are still sailors, happiest at the frontier, same as we all are, and Tromso welcomed the oil men like it had welcomed the whalers before them. After all's said, they are Klondykers, all of them.

You all know sailor's bars, but Tromso is different, I guess. When men have to struggle their way through arctic nights to the warm lights of bars and hotels and they have to put up with nights that last three months at a time, well it changes them, I reckon, and often enough they fight their way to town from the dock through blizzards that blow straight from the pole for days on end.

That's the winter of course, hard and bloody brutal, but summer in Tromso is different. Under the glare of a white night Tromso looks its age. There may be a football stadium outside the town now, and bright neon where the kerosene lamps once burned yellow and smoking in the bar windows, but in the bright light of the polar summer the port looks old. Take away the flattering effect of twilight and the old whaling bases just look dead.

Tromso is like that. In bright light the slips where they dragged giant carcasses seem to be more part of the slaughterhouse than a chapter of a romantic story. In the summer it never gets dark and everything looks it's age in that hard northern light.

Near the end of number two wharf, close by where we moored to take on fuel oil, there was a scrap dump, piled thirty foot high. The Arctic weather had preserved it. The dry winds and bitter cold had slowed rusting to a slow creep. The machines looked as if they had been dumped only yesterday, their paint was still fresh where the winds hadn't had a chance to sandblast the surfaces to bare shiny metal. It felt like Tromso was just biding its time, waiting for us to do the job and be gone, before our equipment was rusting on the pile with the rest, just one more story of frontier man, in a place that had seen enough of such things already.

There was no manned diving that we could do on the wreck. Commosolet is in nearly fifteen hundred metres, a vertical mile of cold water. Down there, under pressures that would crush a man to a tennis ball sized hunk of meat in less time that the thought might take, in darkness that is softened only by the bright glow of the luminous creatures of the deep, was the remains of the Northern fleet's finest. Normally as all of you know very well, finding a modern wreck is not really difficult. The bulk of a steel hull sitting on the abyssal plain makes a target that magnetometer surveys and side scan sonar can pick up in minutes – if, that is, we know roughly where to look.

Commosolet was different. Finding her was a real bitch. Being so very deep, the sonar, which works on reflected undersea echoes, gets fooled by layers of temperature graded waters. Cold water lying under a warm layer can reflect the beam just like a solid target. It's called the 'Bottom Simulating Reflecting Layer' and, as an effect, it's a pain in the arse. I reckon most of you have been on time sensitive jobs when it's fucked things up. Because of that effect, it was getting near the end of the day shift on the third day before we finally got a solid target and the ROV was ready to go down to take a look. And it were then, when the hard work was pretty well done, our support ship turned up, and she was a surprise.

The Russian survey vessel, Mir, was very near a celebrity in her own right, after her starring role in 'Titanic' but the fact is the company that runs her on behalf of the Russian Federation really have no choice about how they work. Built as a survey/deep ocean rescue ship, she were only just ready for sea when the Cold War ended. And most of her work was taken away from her just like that. She could have been one more bit of brilliant technology that got scrapped in the name of glasnost, but, as things worked out, Russian free enterprise took over and offered her on the Spot Market, to anyone who could afford the charter fees. Mir spruced up her sad Soviet image, took on a nice new white paint job, and went to work. Mind you, you could still see the ghost of a hammer and sickle where it had been welded onto her funnel. We knew she was on the market for charter work, but we were still surprised to see her that afternoon. Shit, I mean, it was a Soviet boat we were looking at. I know things change but, twenty years ago Mir would have been interested alright, the way a bloody fox is interested in a goose. Still we are all good friends now, at least as long as there's a profit in it.

Our brief was to look at the wreck by remote. For us it was all ROV work, but Mir's submersible was a lot more useful than a simple ROV. It could take a three man crew down to the wreck to take a close look, and eyes on the bottom are better than any bloody TV camera.

Anyhow, like I said, her arrival caused quite a flap among our crew. Jimmy, our ROV guy, was especially interested. Most ROV men are in love with their remote technology, but Jimmy was the exception. Really, he'd wanted to be a Sat diver, but he hadn't made the medical when it came to it. So he was mad keen for the next best thing. It was his ambition, he would explain to anyone who would listen, to dive in a manned deep water submersible.

This odd ambition confused the hell out of most of us. Submersibles have a wicked reputation after all. It goes right back to the days when the Pisces series of two man subs made a career of getting stuck on the bottom, back in the Klondyke days in the North Sea. Okay, bell divers always look vulnerable on the end of their fifty metres of umbilical, but submersibles killed more men in those early years by far, and, besides, they are buggers to launch, and even harder to recover.

Still deep sea probes like Mir's are another thing again. They are just spheres of titanium alloy with big observation windows. Head on they look like a bloody big grasshopper. They are fitted with a range of manipulators to turn valves or what have you, and they can work very deep. The problem with these things is that if something fails (and we all know fine well that, in the end, failures are pretty well certain to happen), the crew stand virtually no hope of rescue. I reckon the best that they can hope for when it happens is a massive pressure failure, after all that would be quick. Otherwise it's a long slow wait in the cold and the dark 'til the gas runs out. Mir's submersible was Russian gear at its post-Soviet best, but even so, the idea of diving in her didn't appeal to anyone else on board aside from Jimmy. Now most of you are ex-mob and you all know what a nuke can do. We've all seen those creepy films of those wooden ghost towns out in the American deserts. And you get to see what happens when the blast waves hit – that double punch effect when the blast wave hits and then the overpressure falls and the building gets sort of sucked down.

You know what would happen to a city, but you sort of block it out, you know? Even when I were serving on the Trident boats I were sort of blocking out what we were really doing, I mean, carrying the nukes, like. Once, I got to go into the silo. Nothing to see really. Just a lot of steel tubes like the legs on a jacket painted bright white. But I remember thinking that each one of them were a death warrant for three, maybe four, Russian cities. I were married then, Sally had just had our first. It makes you think, you know?

In the end someone on Mir's crew got to know Jimmy in a Tromso bar on one of our port calls, they were Russian of course. It was funny like, drinking with the guys who were our Oppos during the Cold War , we might have been trying to kill each other if things had been a bit different. As it was, we were singing and drinking. Well, like I said, a sailor is a sailor, whoever he works for. Anyhow, to cut a long story short, they offered ROV Jimmy the chance to go down and look at the wreck close to. Mind you, they were savvy enough to make sure he signed a disclaimer to say he were going at his own risk if it all went tits up. So that night, it were still light of course – that twilight you get in the summer up there – the Mir had the submersible on her launching skids out on the aft deck. The dive were scheduled to go at midnight local time. Right on the button Jimmy was sealed up with this pair of big Russian guys from her regular crew. The surface jumpers were already in the inflatable ready to help her launch. They give Jimmy this tablet four hours ahead of the dive to make sure that he wouldn't need to take a crap during the five hours or so of the time underwater. The things we do for England, eh?

Anyhow Jimmy comes out, ready to go aboard, and he's wearing this red Russian jump suit, like them that they use in American prisons. We watched them climb in and the deck crew screwed the hatch tight shut, and the cranes lifted the submersible and lowered her into the water. There's an umbilical of course, but it's really just for surface lifting. Once the sub is in the water, it's on its own. So the surface jumpers climb on the half sunk hull of the sub and they unclamp the lifting lines and she gently sinks into the oggen.

Like always, at first you can see the lights. After they got a few feet deep they turned them on. They are too hot to run them in the air, they'd just cook. So there's this greenish glow and the umbilical snaking down.

It was hanging loose by then, waiting for them to come back. After a bit it's all gone and there's nothing to see from topside but that greenish glow gradually sinking, until after a few minutes, there was nothing to see at all, aside from the odd exhaust bubble breaking the surface. Well, after a half hour or so we reckoned the sub must be getting near the bottom. So then we all went to watch the TV monitors on the repeaters in our dive control, just to see how the dive was going.

First off it was like always. It was same picture you get from an ROV, plankton like a fucking mist to bugger up the visibility then there was an odd fish, bloody odd some of them were too. There are weird things in the deep that far north. Well, after a bit, the wreck shows up. At first there was just a dark shape against the shadows. So the sub went in really slow, then there she was, lying on her side and buried maybe two metres or so into the soft shit on the bottom. First thing you could really make sense of was a prop. It had loads and loads of blades, like all those sub props have. It makes them quieter, cuts out the cavitation noises. This prop was still shiny, I remember, like it had just been fitted in the yard yesterday. All the rest of the hull was covered with those rubbery anti sonar tiles that they plated those boats with, and there was the odd one missing, the bare steel showing through where something had jarred it loose.

The TV picture were a bit jerky, a bit pixelated, the way through water comms always are, and it was black and white. It looked like an old nineteen fifties TV show. They swam along the wreck, past the conning tower, and the lights reflected back off the windows. The TV picture kept burning out in black holes with bright white flares in the centre where the reflections of the submersible's lights off the glass overloaded the picture tubes. In the end they got to the bows – Jesus Christ, lads, she was big, that boat – and they ran well past her out into the dark so as to swing around and come back towards the sub, face to face, so to speak. Finally we were looking at her, bows on, and the wreck was like a bloody great cliff rearing up out of the mud. There were three torpedo tubes on each side of the bow. They were stacked one on top of the other in two lines. Two of the clamshell doors were still clamped shut, the other four were dark circles against the greys of the acoustic tiles. The sub edged closer and the high intensity lighting illuminated the first few feet of the tubes themselves. In one of them a deep water crab – it looked pale like most deep sea creatures – scuttled out of the light into the depths of the torpedo tube getting away from the lights. There was a bright strobe flash as the cameras took a high definition picture for the records, and just for a few moments after that, the burn out blinded the camera that was feeding our TV. Right after that – it was still just audio comms, we had no pictures of the inside of Mir's Sub – things started to go pear shaped big time. First off there was this gabble in Russian. I don't speak a word of Russian aside from 'niet' and 'da', but you don't need to understand a language to realise that someone is in a panic. You all know how it is with crews, it's the one thing you don't do, can't ever afford to do, after all panic is a killer. When the shit hits the fan, the one chance you have of making it through is if every bugger does just what they are supposed to do.

So hearing that gabble over the comms, especially when all we had was sound without the picture, was scary, 'cause we knew right off that something was wrong. There was this one bloke from the Russian marine crew, he could speak good English. Andrei, they called him, big bugger he was, built like a brick shit house, well, he was always happy to talk. Most of them weren't, you know? They still acted as if the bloody Cold War was still going on, and we were, well, not the enemy exactly, but the next best thing to it.

Anyhow, after a bit Andrei comes into the control room and gives us the gen on what's happening. The fact was that that bloody submersible had only done a Pisces and got herself stuck on the bottom without power. The crew were okay for the time being. They'd battery power for twelve hours or more, at least, and as long as the CO_2 scrubbers held out, there was no chance that anything would happen to them, gas wise. Cold was another thing, mind you. Heaters use a lot of battery life and the water temperature that deep is only a few degrees. I'm guessing that as soon as they lost power they got into space blankets to give the best protection they could. We weren't really too worried about them right then. Submersibles are made with this kind of problem in mind and since the Pisces series had all that bother in the seventies there's always been an emergency system. Thing is you could just dump the ballast and go like fuck for the surface but, that said, that's pretty much an uncontrolled situation. The bloody sub could pop up anywhere if you do that, maybe even under the keel of the mother ship. That way you might even sink the two of them. Anyhow, the Russian crew are running around like blue arsed flies and the deck radio working channel was crammed with traffic. We pulled off to standby maybe a half a mile from the Mir, but there wasn't a lot we could do. Our bell and living system were rated to three hundred metres or so but even with a bit of a leeway, assuming our guys were happy to risk it, and a long diver's tether to extend our reach, that bloody submersible was still out of reach. She was just too deep. Besides, if we got to her what the hell could we do? The crane cable wasn't even in the same ball park for length and we had no way to lock onto the stricken sub. The Yanks have a rescue vessel for just this kind of thing but that was on the other side of the world, on exercise in the Pacific. There just wasn't time even if everyone agreed to try using it.

So every bugger is getting nervous by then. The submersible had been down on the bottom for three hours or so, and we knew that they'd be getting cold down there. We had comms back by that point and we could see them on our TV monitors, sitting around in that little bubble under the sea. Not that we really wanted to watch, mind. The picture was dim, 'cause they were using the red emergency lights to save power, but we could see them all wrapped up in space blankets, just waiting.

The Russian engineers shut themselves in the engine room office on the Mir and held a conflab. We could only wait. It seemed like they never would come out. We were sat there waiting to see what they were going to come up with, and all the time, we were thinking that the best that they were going to say was something on the lines of 'Goodbye and thanks for all the fucking fish'.

Anyway, after a bit, the big boss man came up with a blueprint schematic of the sub's wiring, and from it he reckoned he had worked out where the problem was. There was this inspection plate that they could reach from inside the pressure hull where all the wires from the ballast control system ran in a duct. He reckoned all that was needed was to find two particular wires in that duct, strip the insulation and cross connect them with a fly lead, and then, bingo – power. Easy in theory, but remember how fucking cramped those submersibles are and they were working by that dim red light, so fucking good luck checking the colours and tracers on all those wires.

There was nothing we could do but wait and watch. You know, in most of the shit spots I've been in that is the worst bit. It's like just before you go into action. There was this time once in the Falklands thing, I was just a bloody kid then. We knew that the Argies were going to come for us. Two ships were already lost and we were a sitting bloody duck. We could see things going on, on the air defence radar screens and we had just to sit and wait. And, when it did happen, they come in low over the hills to get us on the blind side. Well, it was scary you know, but not as bad as that endless waiting. Nothing is as bad as waiting.

Well, time goes on, we hear fuck all from the submersible and the Russians were saying nothing of course. Remember, lads, we had one of our own stuck in that bloody thing. Then, after three hours or so, we hear on the deck radio that they'd got power back to some of the attitude control systems and she was gradually, so fucking slowly, coming back to the surface. We was lining the rail and watching the sea. More of that bloody waiting – and, after what seemed like forever, we could see that green glow of her strobe beacon flashing away in the dark. By then it was twilight again, and by the time the top side of the sub broke surface it was as dark as it ever gets at that time of the year. There was a cheer from our crew, and bless the straight-faced bastards, the Russians joined in, while the surface jumpers crossed over to her in the Zodiac, and in no time they'd fixed the lifting eye to the shackle on the crane and the submersible was hauled clear of the water and hanging there like something dead, dripping water from all over her.

Well, they got her back onto the deck and opened the hatches, and, one by one, the crew climbed out of the hatch and onto the ladder. ROV Jimmy was the second to come out and he had to be helped to climb down the ladder to the Mir's deck. When that was done and the doctor had checked them all out – no problems there, they were just cold from being without the heaters for so long – anyway Jimmy comes back across to us on the basket and there he is, standing on our deck, looking around as if he couldn't believe he was really there.

We found him a drink to celebrate getting him back in one piece, and inside an hour he was in his pit, so it weren't 'til the morning we got to talk about the dive. I met up with him in the mess that morning. He was sitting there with a mug of coffee like always. So I said "Good to see you safe. Jimmy. Fucking Russian tech, eh?"

He said, "Yeah, Russian fucking tech."

"What was it?" I asked. "Do we know? The failure, I mean?"

"Electrics, I guess," he said. "But that's not the worst of it." Then he said, "Look, there's something else. The thing is, when we were down there, this Russian pilot, well, he was once in their submarine fleet. You got to remember that we thought, just for a bit, that there was no chance of us getting back? People talk more than they should in that situation, say things that normally they wouldn't. Well, it was when we saw them clamshell doors were open, you know, on the Commosolet?"

"Yeah," I said. "We saw that from the TV image."

"Yeah. But you don't know about the fail safe, do you?"

"Sure I do," I said. "Everyone knows about fail safe. It's a system on nukes that means if things go wrong they can't explode. They can't arm. They always fail safe."

"Yeah," said Jimmy as if I'd said something really stupid. "That's how we work but on Russian subs the nukes on those torpedoes work another way. You know we have to arm our gadgets each time we go to firing ready?"

"Sure," I said.

"Well," he said, "the Russians reckoned that for torpedoes, the response time is so short – thing is, it was a theory dreamed up by some old bugger who had served in World War Two – on one occasion he nearly gets killed by a Nazi destroyer 'cause they were too slow to fire. So he reckons that they could save a few seconds by linking the fail safe cut outs to the clamshells. That way as soon as the doors were open, you were good to go. Their idea of fail safe was that both the captain and a senior officer had to give the go code, other than that the gadget was live."

"So those tubes down there…" I said.

"Are loaded with live nukes, yeah."

"Fuck me," I said. I was sort of a bit took aback by the thought.

"Thing is," he said, "what happens now?"

And of course nothing did happen. The whole bloody thing was quietly forgotten once the survey was done. Officially the wreck was surveyed and judged safe to be left where she was. Just to prove the point she was designated a war grave. That way no one can touch her even if we get better at very deep water work.

But for ROV Jimmy it was more personal. See, he was married to a Norwegian lass. Kari, she was called, pretty little woman, loved the bloody bones of the nutty little geek she did. The thing is they lived on the coast just a little away from Stoltenburg base, in a little village perched right on the edge of the ocean. And I could see what he was thinking right off. Those warheads were maybe like ours. Well, the ones that they used on our Ikara system had a blast radius under water of six and half kilometres. Jimmy's family place was maybe eight k from that wreck site. So you see, even if nothing did happen… never mind if one of the warheads went, and if the explosion busted open that fragile reactor containment… Funny how it gets personal sometimes, just when you think it's just another job…

CHAPTER SEVEN

Ever since the cumbersome, romantic and inefficient majesty of sail gave way to the ruthless efficiency of mechanical power, ships have had a weak point. Delivering all that power to the paddle wheels or propeller, demanded, from the very beginning, a way to transmit power through the hull of the ship from the prime mover to the means of propulsion. In the days of sail, a ship's hull was solid, unbroken, a wooden wall against the violence of the sea outside. But the introduction of drive shafts changed all of that.

Very early on, engineers developed ways of carrying a fast spinning steel shaft through a ship's hull without allowing water to make the return trip. Shaft glands, originally nothing more than oil soaked leather washers, gradually developed into a complex and elegant set of seals that actively shoved water back and prevented flooding.

The problem is that, the more complex the gland becomes, the more it tends, over the years, to develop leaks. It is a normal part of maintaining a ship at sea. Every few years, at her dry dock refit, the shaft glands are tested and parts are replaced and seals overhauled, eventually reducing that weak point to a simple, if essential, part of the vessel's regular maintenance schedule.

In her incarnation as The Lady of the Isles, the San Fong had gone through that regular service schedule. Every few years, working to a set routine that depended on how many hours her engines had run, she was inspected by experts from Lloyd's or the Norwegian DNV and certified fit for another year at sea. If there was wear on a critical component it was repaired or replaced, and for twenty four years, it was a regime that kept her safe. Then she came south.

In Indonesia the test regime was relaxed, testing was on a variable, and wholly inefficient, schedule. Certification was often provided on a 'brown envelope' basis in a local restaurant, without the certifying authorities ever seeing the ship, and, on the San Fong, down in the distant recesses of the prop shaft tunnel, where no man ever went without a very good reason, the starboard shaft gland began to leak.

It was nothing to be afraid of, that leak, at least, not at first. The bilge pumps routinely cut in as the water level in the void below the engine room chequer plates rose to their pre-set level, but eventually, down there in the oily darkness, the pump filters began to choke, blocked with waste papers and mousse, that greasy water and heavy oil emulsion, that seems to find the lowest point in every ship, to gather and fester away by itself. That night, the night of the typhoon, the pumps were getting close to the limits that they could handle. Finally, stressed beyond the limits of design, they ground to a halt.

Ninety feet above, on the open decks of the ferry where the tropical air was already saturated with moisture, and the heat lightning was crackling away in the distance, a hundred and fourteen deck passengers, the poorest of the San Fong's complement, watched the gathering elements with a degree of apprehension that was gradually edging towards fear.

At the aft end of the deck, in the shelter of a winch whose glossy green paint job was the newest thing about it, Sue Fangsu, Anglo-Chinese, daughter of a Malay whore and a Danish ship's cook, was huddled against the heat and the flickering blue flashes that played on the near horizon.

She was on the ferry because she was running away. Where she was running to, seemed, at the time, not to matter greatly, so long as it was somewhere away from Miss Christina's bar, where she had sold herself two or three times a night for the last eight years.

There was nothing really special about her, just the routine tragedy of an unwanted girl child born into a society where she had only one readily saleable asset. Her mother had sold her for the first time when she was just twelve years old. The client had been a fat jolly Malay businessman, and he had made her laugh and given her presents and it was all fine, until the night he had decided to make good on his investment, and raped her, raped her hard without any kind of preliminary at all, holding one soft hand over her mouth to stifle the screams. That first time it had seemed to last forever, and afterwards, when it was over, her mother had given her fifty dollars in cash and told her that she had done well. She never saw the businessman again – his interest only extended to that first experience, and, with that done, done and paid for, she was just one more street kid growing up in a world where she was a commodity, and nothing more.

She had drifted into Christina's bar and worked from there, because there, at least, there she had a room, and a bed, and she was no longer forced to work in the teeming alleys. Christina's was better. Well, it was less totally degrading at least. When she was seventeen she became pregnant for the fifth time. The first four times she had talked to the oldest of Christina's whores and explained her predicament. Western medicine had provided an answer in the shape of three little pills taken twice a day for a week. There were cramps at first, then a little pain, and, eventually, a smear of blood that signalled the uneventful end of another potential life. The last time she had fallen pregnant she had tried the pills but nothing happened. Nothing that is, aside from a massive bout of vomiting and a severe backache and, somehow, the fact that the foetus had hung on in there, despite the best efforts she could make to dislodge it, touched her emotionally in a way that no one had touched her in years. All that time she had cut herself off from feeling anything at all, turning her face aside from each new encounter, isolating her sensations from even the most intimate of contact. Even when she had contracted an STD for the first time, courtesy of a Yugoslav sailor who smelled of old onions, she had kept that thick mental carapace intact, isolating the real inner being from the body it inhabited. Now, from this totally unexpected direction, she felt the first stirrings of maternal love and, in her loveless life, it was devastating in its intensity. The older women had been at first sympathetic, and then, as she made her intention of going through with the pregnancy clear, they had become, first incredulous, and then, increasingly irritated. For them, the one chance of escape that they dreamed of, the rich client who would take them from Christina's bar and keep them in idleness, was a comforting mirage, as long as it never materialised. A child did not fit that dream, and never could. In the end, one night when the skies were dark with the approaching typhoon, and the air was even more heavy than usual, Sue Fangsu packed her few belongings into a soft bag, added the pathetic small cache of worn bank notes that she had squirrelled away over the years, and left for the wharf where the ferry San Fong was waiting.

CHAPTER EIGHT

Around the same time that the all 'be aware' met call was going out, Billy Knowles, the system tech, on the Typhoon Star, was beginning a tale of a shipwreck. Sailors have always told such stories, ranging from the fearsome Dutch captain who cursed God and was condemned to fight the screaming hell of Cape Horn through all eternity, to contemporary sightings of phantom oil platforms and mighty super tankers that vanish from radar as abruptly as they had once vanished from the ken of mortal man. There are always tales of the supernatural and macabre.

Sailors are superstitious, maybe because, like actors, that other notably superstitious profession, a sailor's whole life is surrounded, always, by the workings of random chance. The time that lies between a placid uneventful voyage and a disaster at sea can be as short as a few seconds.

So it was with the incinerator ship Vulcan. She was a ship better known among sailors by her reputation, than from direct experience, but, alone of those on the Star, Billy Knowles had once actually sailed on her.

"It was more or less routine," he said. "We always joined her at sea, if you see what I'm telling you. The thing was the Vulcan, well, she were always working on the fucking edge. We was never really outside the law, but then, we weren't exactly inside it either…"

Billy — the system tech

I know none of yous have ever worked her, or any other incinerator ship for that matter, but you all know well enough what's needed. With all the green regs that everyone has to stick by nowadays, well, there's loads of stuff to get rid of that no bugger is too keen on dealing with.

So, the Vulcan. When I joined her, they'd ripped out almost all her works below decks. She started as an old reefer, if you see what I'm telling you, and they put out all the cold store gear and put in three bloody great burners, looked like old fashioned bottle kilns they did. You'll know what I mean if you ever visited the five towns around Stoke and the old potteries district. My dad's mother came from there, and I remember the incinerators on the Vulcan were that exact same shape. On the Vulcan they ran from tank top level right up to the stacks that opened way above the bridge like three fucking great chimneys sticking up through the deck, which I guess they was, if you see what I'm telling you.

All we done, all we ever done on that boat was to meet with a tanker, well out to sea somewhere, usually it were in international waters, and well away from the coast. Well, they'd pump the shit into our holding tanks down below decks, whatever it happened to be, and it were a bloody performance sometimes. We'd be wearing full contamination suits and breathing gear, this was just to load the cargo, mind, and then, when it were all loaded, we'd feed it into the burners.

We had this two man team of scientists on board, they were supposed to check each load and work out how best to treat it. Mind you, I never saw them reject a load all the time I was aboard.

Anyhow, it got fed to the burners. They ran bloody hot those burners. Oxy-hydrogen they ran on. We'd take anything, no matter how evil it might be, and turn it to gas and ashes. Now the thing is and always was, that no company fed its wastes to the fucking Vulcan if there were a cheaper way, so what we got was often the really bad shit. I did hear that after the chemical weapons ban come in, most of the stuff that suddenly no bugger wanted, went up our stacks, but I can't swear to that, if you see what I'm telling you.

Anyhow, the burners. If you've never seen one, there was this bloody great cone shape that started out wide at the base and tapered off as it went up towards the stacks. You pumped in gases at the bottom, oxy-hydrogen like I said, bloody hot stuff that was, and then, a bit higher up the stack you sprayed in the crap you were burning. The idea was it was so bloody hot in there that everything burned away to nothing.

The thing is all that heat were a problem. So to keep things hot and not to waste fuel, the burners were insulated with a thick coat of asbestos plaster. Course, that's the same shit that has killed more laggers than you could shake a bloody stick at, but there it was, as thick as a man's forearm is long, and under that layer there was the steel of the burner itself, and inside that a fire brick lining before you got to the inside of the furnace itself. It was all good for the five trips that I worked on her, but for one thing.

There was this hot spot on the side of number three burner. Well, I mean the whole bloody burner deck was hotter than the fires of hell, but there was this bit of the casing that was a lot more than just warm. Now we reported it to the engineers, but no bugger gave much of a tin fuck for what the bloody operators had to say so... well, I'm guessing here, but I reckon that, what was going on, was that the flame jet from the burners was not burning straight, so it was heating a patch of the fire brick lining. Now we're talking oxy-hydrogen, boys, if you understand what I'm telling you, and, sure enough, after a while that hot spot was hot enough to melt the firebrick lining to fucking glass. Then the flame starts playing on the steel casing itself and that lasts no more than a few hours before it melts through, and suddenly, all that stood between the inside of the burner and the inside of the

45

fucking ship, was a bit of asbestos insulation. First we knew was when the alarms went off – too fucking late by then, boys – all we could do was shut off the fuel and hope.

Well, two hours after the flame burned through we were all, well, those of us what survived were at least, in a fucking Watercraft lifeboat, bobbing about and watching while what was left of the ship settled into the water. It took a good long time, lads, ships are slow to die most times, as you all know well enough but, in the end, there's a big rumble like a loud fart in the water and a bubble of gas comes up. And then she was gone, and there was just these three boats in the middle of a patch of Southern Ocean.

Well, you all know what it's like in that sort of situation. If there's a man here who can say he has never been adrift in a lifeboat, even if it were a practice, I'll call him a liar. We were in the boats for two days, more or less, and out of the three boats that started out we lost touch with two on the second night, when the weather came up the way it does down in the south. I were lucky. I were in boat three and we came through with no worse than a few cuts and bruises to show. Mind you, we nearly lost the mate to sea sickness, poor sod. We was picked up by an Australian research ship that had followed the distress signal from our beacon all the way to us. They never did find the other two boats though, nor the forty three men who had been in them. Later, it were a long time after, the fuss had gone back a bit. I got talking to an engineer from a Met service boat that went around servicing the big monitor buoys out in the empty bit. It was him told me what happened after. They got this radar ping one morning, Thing was, they was looking for a buoy that had broken loose and gone walkabout, so the first idea was that that was it. But when they comes up on it, well, it weren't a buoy at all, but a Watercraft lifeboat, and going by the state of the stuff growing on the hull it had been adrift a bloody good long time. They pulls up alongside it. As it happens the sea was quiet and they managed to snag the boat alright, but when they lowered a ladder and climbed aboard it and hammered on the decking there was no sign of life. They opened the hatch and sure enough, there was our missing crew, what was left of them at any rate.

The guy I had the story from said that they weren't rotten or nothing, just dried out like those old Egyptian mummies you see photos of. There wasn't nothing to be done for them, so they took what ID they could off the bodies and used a little demolition charge to sink that old water craft so it wouldn't float about and be a problem if someone hit it.

They read the service over the spot and wrapped them in canvas, sailor style. After they'd had themselves that bit of a service, they deep sixed the lot of 'em. After all, they were three months out from the next landfall and no one wanted thirty odd dead ones aboard for all that time. Most of 'em were identified by the numbers on their survival suits. No wonder we calls them body bags. Makes you think, don't it? If you see what I'm saying to you.

CHAPTER NINE

As Billy finished his story, the starboard shaft gland on the San Fong, then three hundred nautical miles from the Star, suffered an increased water leak that went from a drip to a trickle, and then to a steady pressurised spray of sea water.

Under better circumstances, even this would have been nothing more than an inconvenience, just something to be noted and corrected at the next scheduled maintenance and refit docking, but thanks to the combination of the non-functioning bilge pumps and the non-indicating water level tell tales that had allowed the situation to develop unnoticed, the situation was rapidly shifting from annoying to dangerous.

Small faults should never be knowingly left uncorrected. On a ship at sea, far from help, that much is axiomatic. But to correct a fault, one must first be aware that the fault exists. On the bridge control panel below and to the right of the compass tell tale dial, there was a long line of green lit panels. Each one was more or less three centimetres square and each one was neatly labelled. The panel of lights was directly below the helmsman's field of vision as he stood at the controls. There was no ship's wheel as such on the San Fong. She was an old ship, but not that old, all the essential control functions ran from a simple joystick.

All the tell tale indicators lights glowed a steady, and comforting, green. The rows of red tell tales below, a dark twin of the 'all's well' panel, stayed dark. Andy had no way of knowing that the tell tales were lying and that, deep below, four decks below bridge deck level, the sea was invading his ship, stealthily creeping in, eroding the narrow margin of safety that lay between her and the storm.

There was no real warning at first, outside of the most subtle signs. It began with a slight sluggishness in her handling. It was nothing that a landsman would have even noticed. It was just a slight reluctance to answer the helm rapidly. There was long period when, even at that stage, with the ship taking on water, the situation might have been saved, but when the tipping point moment finally came, it escalated from trivial to disastrous in minutes.

On the bridge a single green light on the panel flickered and went out. A moment later the light below it flickered and lit up a baleful red. Simultaneously, a klaxon added its raucous scream to the racket of the gathering storm outside. On the San Fong the time of the nightmare was come. The rising water level down below had reached the one working sensor that was left and it was that last line of defence that finally tripped an alarm. It was all far too late.

Andy's response was textbook – the response of a professional sailor. It took perhaps five seconds for him to make a decision, and then he hit the manual over-ride that should have started the bilge pumps. There was no response. The control lights that indicated the status of the bilge pumps remained obstinately dark. Andy thumped the panel with a flat hand as if that might start the reluctant pump, and lacking any response to that, he picked up the engine room telephone.

"Chang," he said, without any preliminary, 'I've got water in the bilges and no response from the pumps on my panel. Get someone into the void space to find out what the hell is going on, Mister."

Andy knew right then that this was not going to be a routine breakdown. The gathering storm, and the increasing decrepitude of this old boat, was telling him so. He put the telephone back on its rest and then thought for a moment more. On the San Fong the Radio Room was directly off the bridge. Andy had only to raise his voice to make himself heard.

"Sparks," he said, in the tone of a man commenting on the weather on an English summer's day. "I'm declaring a 'pan' call. Get it out on an 'all ships', will you?"

The 'pan' call is one stage below a full 'mayday'. It warns all shipping in the immediate area of a troubled ship that a situation has developed that might need a full scale rescue. Three hundred miles to the west, at the very limit of the radio call, the signal from the ferry, weak and attenuated by the electrical activity of the storm, reached the Typhoon Star and triggered a well worn and long practised response.

The Star's radio room was equipped far more lavishly than the average merchant ship, as a result of the total dependence of salvage crews on their communications. At need, incoming radio calls to a salvage vessel can be routed to the ship's PA system so that every member of the crew is kept aware of a developing situation. It is part of the operating system of salvage crews, and by that means every man aboard, from steward to first mate, is kept abreast of developments as they happen. The effect of that sharing of information is that the crew work as a well oiled, tight knit team.

Down in the Star's dive control room the tannoy crackled into life. Conversations fell silent, everyone simply listened.

"All hands," said the anonymous voice from above, "all hands, be aware that we have picked up a 'pan pan' call from a ferry some distance from us. At the moment, the call remains at that low level, but possibly escalating, status. All section leaders take appropriate action please. Any further incoming comms from the possible casualty will be relayed via ship's pipes as the messages are received, thank you."

The possibility of an extra job, with the prospect of prize money, in addition to already generous basic pay, had an immediate effect on the gathering in the control room. Real life is rarely dramatic, there is no 'standby for action stations' on a salvage tug, no 'general quarters' alarm.

Salvage, by long tradition, is the only remaining sector of an increasingly professional industry that still lives by rules that are little changed since the days of the eighteenth century privateers. A salvage boat, at the discretion of the master of the tug and the agreement of the master of the casualty craft, may agree to a Lloyd's Open Agreement. This rather weird form of contract states that the salvor must use all 'due measures' and 'best efforts' to rescue the ship in difficulty. For this service he may claim a proportion of the value of the rescued ship and the cargo, if any, usually fixed by negotiation with the insurers. No legal pressure or obligation is placed on the salvor to protect life. That, rather quaintly, is regarded only as the duty of the brotherhood of the ocean. The Lloyd's Open has a real benefit for salvors, offering, as it does, a pay day far and away more lucrative than any contract they might arrange, but it also has a sting in the tail that has been the downfall of many a salvor. The Lloyd's Open has a 'no cure/ no pay' clause, and that is as inflexible as the salvor's right to an inflated fee. If, under the terms of no cure/no pay, a salvor fails to rescue the casualty, if he fails to take the damaged ship to a safe port, then, no matter what costs the salvor incurs in the course of the job, no matter how dangerous it turns out to be, even if the salvage ship herself is lost in the course of the rescue, the owners have no recourse in law.

Even this piratical agreement is an improvement on the older system. Under the old laws of salvage, a ship in difficulties became a derelict and the property of anyone who could secure a line to her. But only if there was no living thing left aboard her, not even a ship's dog. For two hundred years before Lloyds decided, in their wisdom, that the insurance industry was acting as an unwilling accessory to murder, this rule led to salvage operations being very close to legalised wrecking, and many a poor shipwrecked soul made it ashore through the raging surf only to be met with a mob intent on salvage, who could only legally claim the goods that they took by making quite certain that no member of that crew survived the wreck.

The only surviving remnant of those times is the allocation of prize money, whereby the salvage ship's crew are paid a bonus according to the value of the prize. On a percentage basis each man gets a slice of the pot after the ship's expenses are paid. The rate is strictly based on the ship's management structure. It is a system that traces back as far as the buccaneers, the seventeenth century 'brotherhood of the coast' when each man, before the division of loot was made, swore that he had held back not a 'pennyworth' of booty from the communal horde.

Three percent for a medium level deckhand may not sound a lot, but, when the prize is worth millions, the cash value adds up. Because of all this, the atmosphere in the little gathering in the control room was almost party-like at that stage. That said, until the final decision to make a salvage attempt was made, there was nothing to do but wait.

CHAPTER TEN

Chris Johanssen's only outward sign of excitement at the news was an increasing frequency of drags on his malodorous home roll. He was an old hand at this game and had, by all accounts, a long history of skirting the rule of law since his time in an armed forces jail in the eighties. Chris had the build of a fire plug, and the look of a bar room brawler. There was a long white scar running down his left cheek, livid against the habitual tan of a long time deep sea sailor, but, within the scary exterior, there was the soul of a poet. On his off time he read voraciously. Endless books on philosophy with occasional forays into theology. It was not the reality (or otherwise) of God that really interested Chris, it was the complexity of debate, the mental contortions of syntax and logic. It was the sheer, intellectual challenge of debate that struck him as worthwhile.

In many ways, the man was a paradox of the kind that is common enough at sea. Chris was a son of a Yorkshire mining village in the north of the UK who had faced a set of stark choices when the local pit collapsed after Arthur Scargill's unwise attempt at muscular trade union activity, ran up against a national leader who was even more unbending than he was.

Chris had gone from a certain, if hard working future in the pit, to a totally bleak outlook of no work, no hope, and no chances. He drifted through a series of petty criminal activities, selling drugs to bored clients who were even more without hope than he was, ending as a small time dealer before, finally, it became obvious that in the end the local police would settle his future by way of a conviction that would hang over him like a bad smell, and a long prison sentence,

Chris joined the army not because he was especially warlike but because it was a certain route to employment and there were very few of them in his life. Eventually, finding his attitude uncooperative at best, the army parked him in the detention centre at Aldershot where discipline was harsh and mainly mindless. Chris was not impressed by the experience, but it had a single useful outcome. During one long endless session of routine exercise he had fallen in with a simian little man called Jock Wilson whose interest in the army was marginally less than Chris's own.

This man, like many aimless men of no real talent, had a dream. He had heard by various grapevine routes that a man could go into the offices of the French Legion De'tranger and sign up under a new name with a new identity, shedding his past and becoming who ever he chose to be.

Months later, after a trip across France that was mainly by thumb and the occasional coach, Chris Griffiths walked into the office of the Legion on the Rue Maison Bleu in Marseilles. An hour later Chris Johannsen, a new man with a new identity and French nationality was born. His first name he kept unchanged according to the Legion's own regulations. Johannsen he adopted from a notorious porn Star. Chris had loved the Legion. True, the discipline was harsh and the pay barely adequate but it was a true adventure that took him wherever French influence had reached during the days of empire. Finally, nearing the end of his second five year stretch, he had found himself in a village somewhere in West Africa.

It was one more dirty African war where both sides were dragged into more and more extreme methods by circumstance. Chris's own long distance patrol group, operating well inside bandit country had come across a village where the old had been butchered and the young enslaved or murdered depending on their age and perceived level of attraction. Feelings even among Chris's hard-bitten set of professionals, were running high. When they first reached Busissiwe village, just another wide spot in a bush track, the village was still smouldering. Clearly the enemy force was not far ahead of them.

Finally, three kilometres down the trail, they came upon an ambush. It was set at a second village that was not even a wide place in the road. There was in fact no real road in any case, just a dusty goat track leading to a collection of rough buildings constructed from fawn mud bricks. The first burst of automatic fire came from the cover of one of them.

To take on a professional Legion patrol group in such a fashion was a suicide mission. Chris's group fell back to cover and returned fire with automatic weapons and RPGs. The burst from the first rocket grenade reduced the building that was the source of the incoming fire to rubble and dust. There were a couple of bundles of rags in the debris and no sign of life. To be certain, Chris himself hosed them with a long burst from his carbine then the group spread out to make a more diffuse target and advanced on the village.

In such circumstances, small events can trigger massive responses. The flicker of movement at the doorway of one of the remaining huts was enough. Chris's number two, a young recruit who called himself Pierre, screamed, "Contact," and cut loose a burst of 5.62 rounds in the general direction of the hut. Instantly responding, the rest of the group piled in with three rocket propelled grenades that flew in woolly, greasy trails of exhaust smoke, and reduced the hut to a heap in a few white flashes and total carnage. It was only after the smoke cleared, and they were investigating the kill, that they found the eight children, or at least parts of them. They had been sheltering in the hut and moved at the wrong moment. One severed arm with an intact hand held a stick with a white rag fixed to it. There were no weapons, no trace of warlike activity, just dead children and rubble.

Chris's interest in a career in warfare more or less evaporated after that. He still went about his duties, he remained the good soldier he had always been, but the certainty, the certainty of being on the side of right, rather than being part of the forces that were dragging mankind back towards the cave again, that was gone. Up to that moment he had never seen himself as one of the bad guys, always, he had thought, deep down, that the Legion was on the side of right. Certainly, they used force, but only to further the greater good. Killing children was not compatible with that, no matter.

A few months later, with his final contracted stretch over, Chris left the Legion, handed in his personal kit for one final time and walked into the offices of Comex Diving that as it happened was no more than a half kilometre away. His intention was no more focused than temporary employment while he cast around for something more permanent and the Legion had taught him basic diving skills as part of an ordnance disposal course.

And that was how, via a very long convoluted time, Chris Johanssen, ten years afterwards, found himself on the Star.

"Odd that you should mention dreams," he said, between drags on his home roll, as if he were contemplating a great inner vista. "There was a time when I got into Indian religions in a big way. It was the eighties and I was young enough then to think that there were really 'answers' out there to the big questions, you know?"

There was a general murmur of agreement around the control room, not that any of the crew, aside from Chris himself, had any real interest in philosophy. In fact hardly anyone on the Star really knew anything about his background, he was simply accepted as all good workers are accepted at sea. As to his interest in the big questions, the crew simply accepted that along with everything else. Even so they all recognised the folly of youth, and of course everyone accepted that Chris could tell a good tale. In the closed environment of a ship at sea that was a valuable ability.

"We were working out of Cochin," he said. "Bloody odd place that is at the best of times. It just doesn't seem to really have become Indian again after the Portuguese finally left. Then there's the spice market of course. I used to enjoy wandering around it, looking at all the baskets of spices, just sitting there, and listening to the traders doing their best to sell you something. There was this one place…"

Chris – Deputy Rescue coordinator

It was a bit off the main drag, down this little alley where you could near as dammit touch both walls if you stood in the middle of the alley with your arms held out to the sides. It was a bit scary really. If you were on your own especially, there being no room to do anything but fight it out if things turned nasty. Still, this was Cochin, not Juhu or a favela in Rio, and most of the local bad lads in Cochin are no more than chancers who bugger off if you so much as growl at them. It wasn't the sort of place where you might find a man with a gun anyhow, and, well, fuck it, lads, I liked the place. Anyhow there was this – well, I suppose you'd call it a shop. It was just this dingy little room right off the alley. There was a bit of light, just a bare bulb on a bit of wire hanging in the middle of the room. It was darkish too, the whole place was half in shadow so you could barely see the stuff he was selling. Besides, whatever you moved so you could get a good look at something, well, some bloody thing with loads of legs would run out from under it. It got so you'd shift a bit of stuff and wait while the resident wildlife buggered off before you took a good look. Then there was the stock. It was like the souvenir joints you find in Mumbai, you know the ones down in the Chor Bazaar. There's loads of stuff on offer there that is no more Indian than I am, and most of it only ten minutes old.

Anyhow, that was this shop in a back street in Cochin. I only once saw the old guy who owned the place. He was talking to this pair of young Yank girls in tops so thin they were bloody near see through. I watched while he sold them this statue of Ganesh. All brass it was, and a bloody rough bit of casting, even by Indian standards. Well, he tells them that it was from a temple, and he reckoned that it must be at least three hundred years old. This is a statue, mind you, that looked like it came out of the foundry yesterday. Then, to add insult to injury, he says that, of course they'd need paperwork to get it past customs at the airport. But then, he said, that was okay, he was happy to provide it. So he sells them this worthless bit of junk for about two hundred bucks, and on top of that, he sells them a bit of paper with Hindi text on it and tells them it was proof that they were the proper owners, and that they had been cleared by the Department of Antiquities to take it out of the country, and he charges them another hundred for that. God knows what that paper was – neither one of them could read it, so it might as well have been a flyer from the local flea pit advertising the latest Hindi film, or a workshop manual for a bullshit machine for all I know.

Well, all I'm saying is that I've seen the tourist rip offs all over the place, and, I'm no expert, but I can surely tell the real shit from the sauerkraut by now. So, there I was, looking around this little place in Cochin, and then I got a glimpse of a little bronze figurine in the shadows. Now that one was bronze by the look of it, and it had that dark brown colour you only get with old pieces that have never been cleaned. It looked a bit like a standard statue of dancing Shiva but this one wasn't shown dancing in a wheel of fire like the tourist pieces always are. This was just a dancing figure standing on one foot on a round base, but there was an odd thing about it. You know the story of Shiva's third eye? No? Well the Hindu Mystics say that if you go into trance and say Shiva's name over and over, like a mantra, in the end he will open his third eye and destroy all of creation. That's a nice idea, isn't it? Anyhow, all the statues you ever find of Shiva show his third eye closed tight. This statuette had that third eye wide open. There was something else about that little figure that was different. It wasn't tourist shit for a start. Whatever else it was, that statue was the real thing. It was not some casting that had been churned out by the million by the foundry in Mumbai. Course, as soon as I set eyes on it, I knew I wanted to own it.

So I did the usual haggle with the old bugger who ran the place. He was wrinkled and creased. It was hard to think how old he might be. He looked like a dark-skinned old monkey with bright little black eyes looking out of this wrinkled face. That was the first odd thing, looking back, normally you have to argue over every fucking cent, but he just seemed to go through the motions of haggling. It was as if he wasn't really trying, and in the end, I walked out with the figure wrapped up in a bit of old newspaper.

I put it on the desk in my cabin, and, when it was cleaned up, it looked the business. Well, so far, so good, but, right from the off, it was all a bit odd. That's why you mentioning dreams reminded me. I've never dreamed much, you know? I mean, I know they say that dreams are your mind processing all the new information from the day before, but, well either I don't process much, or on the other hand maybe I have a really boring life.

Anyhow I don't dream much, like I said, or I hadn't until then. Well, I'd had that statue on my desk for a few days, when the dreams started. I say dreams. It was always the same dream really, and after the first few times, I sort of knew what was going to happen, right from the second when the dream started. Not that knowing what was going to happen helped. Even though I knew it was going to be bad, I couldn't break out of the dream.

It always started the same way. I was standing in an empty desert landscape with a bit of a breeze ruffling up the sand around my feet, and there was this feeling that this was a really bad place. You've all been in real life bad spots, I know. The bar you walk into and sit down with your drink, before you realise that the locals are all gathered in a group and standing between you and the way out. The oil fire that won't go out, no matter how hard your firefighting crew work it, or maybe the gas leaking into a confined space, so you know just know that one spark will blow you to hell and gone, and your mate is about to turn on the power switch.

You've all been there. It's just the usual things in life really, that's part of going to sea, part of the deal you take when you sign articles for the very first trip, but that's just fear, you know how I mean? Just old fashioned, self-preservation fear. This dream, it was different fear. This was the thing itself, and it makes your belly go weak like you might shit yourself, and your heart beat feels like it's going at three hundred a minute and there's like a hard lump in your throat that won't let you breathe properly. That's real fear and this dream was like that.

The silly thing was there was nothing obvious to be scared of, there was just this empty desert with this breeze blowing across it, with little dust devils breezing past. There was this smudge in the sky. Like something half seen, low down on the skyline as if something was there that I couldn't quite resolve into a shape. But I couldn't shake this feeling of dread that went with it.

After a few moments of that, in the dream, I could make out a huge eye in the sky, a closed eye with an eyelid that flicked the way that you do, just before you open your eyes after a long sleep. As the flicker settled into a slightly open lid that showed a crescent of eye behind it, this red glare showed. It was as if there was a bright and banked up fire in there, and then, just as it looked as if the eye would finally open, I managed to break the spell and I woke up in my own bunk lying on that narrow mattress that was soaked with sweat.

All of that was certainly not good, but, worse than that, was that every time I had the dream, and, towards the end, that it was very near every night, that eye opened just a little bit more.

It sounds like nothing especially scary, just telling you about it here. After all, it was just a set of dreams that kept happening night after night. But the idea got into my head and I couldn't seem to shake it, that the longer I kept the figurine the more likely it was, that, in the end, the eye would open and I would get to see whoever or whatever owned it, and I really didn't want to see that.

I thought about it, and we were still alongside in Cochin at that point, scheduled to sail three days later. In the end I decided that the best way to put my mind at rest was to take the bloody thing back to the place I'd got it from. After all, the cost was damn all, just a few bucks. So, I wrapped it up and went ashore with my little parcel wrapped in newspaper. It was just like when I had bought the fucking thing. Well, I said fuck all to anyone and I walked right from the dock to the spice bazaar. It was all the same as ever, with those baskets of bright coloured spices and that scent of curry plant in the air. But try as I might, I couldn't find that bloody shop.

There were dozens of little alleys off the main drag but I knew well enough where I'd been before. There was this place on the corner that sold saffron in big glass jars that were full of those orange strands of crocus stamens and it was run by this skinny little Indian woman in a bright red sari. I recognised her for sure 'cause she sort of appealed to me, the way some girls do, just my type, I reckon. In any case there was no alley beside her shop. There was no alley within a few hundred metres of it. That whole long section backed onto a big temple, and there was no way through back there except into the temple complex courtyards, and that was surrounded by a colonnade of pillars. There was no one selling anything there, certainly no poorly lit little curio shop with an old man running it.

I asked the locals but you know the way they blank you if it suits them. It was like I was asking for the way to somewhere dodgy, maybe the local brothel or whatever. Anyhow I took that bloody statuette back to my cabin and put it back on the desk. I reckon that most of you are sitting there thinking why all the fuss? After all, most of you would have just chucked the bloody thing in the gash and forgotten it. But I just couldn't somehow.

The thing is, the statue was so bloody well made, the casting was so good, I just couldn't simply sling it. Besides... well, I just couldn't chuck it out like a bit of shit, but the dreams kept happening, that was the thing. It was every bloody night. It got to the point where I was getting sloppy at the job 'cause I wasn't getting enough sleep. In the end I asked the medic for some stuff to help. He gave me Valium and it did help for a bit, but with the pills, when the dreams started, I couldn't wake up, so I'm just trapped in that nightmare. So even though it made me sleep better in one way, it made things worse in another. Finally there came one night shift, it was deadly quiet, nothing happening, and there was a moon that night, a great big yellow full moon riding on the horizon line and throwing a long track across the water. It was a really lovely night.

Then it happened, up in the dark sky, instead of the moon being a solid yellow globe, the way it always is, instead I thought I saw an eye, just for a second it was, but that was bloody long enough I can tell you. Just for that moment I was back inside the dream, but this time there was no way that I was going to wake up. It just lasted for a second or two, then everything was back to normal. The sky was just the tropical night sky and the moon was just the same old moon, like always. No all seeing eye, just the moon and the stars dusting across the dark where you can see the edge of the galactic lens, just like always, same old sky, same old moon. But shit, I was scared. I remember it so clearly, there was a bit of a flap on among the Indian crew 'cause it was that weekend that Pakistan detonated their first nuke. There was a lot of ugly shit going round, all that crap about how the Muslims had got the bomb. I expect that north of the fucking border it was much the same 'cept up there they were saying that Hindus have got a bomb. Sometimes I wonder about fucking people.

Anyhow that night, after my watch was done, I sat looking at that bloody statue with the sun coming up outside. I wasn't really thinking that it was the gods, Shiva or otherwise that were causing the dreams. I don't believe in the after life, or the occult for that matter, but, I tell you this, I was certain that I was losing my grip on reality. I went to the medic, and told him what was going on, well, part of it in any case, but you could see he couldn't make sense of it. So the best he could do was suggest I took the next tour of duty off, so that maybe the rest at home, away from the job, would help. So I did as I was told like a good little lad, left the bloody statue on my desk in my cabin, flew back to the UK and said nothing to anyone.

Well, come the next tour, it was a full two months later. I'd had no bother in the UK. I slept like a dream so to speak, and the girlfriend never mentioned anything odd happening at night, well, no more than the usual at least. When I got back to India I was feeling great, back to my old self, ready to take on anything, but when I saw that bloody statue still sitting on the desk just the way I'd left it, it was like I'd never left. I felt like the bloody thing was waiting for me.

Next night the dream came back just like before but maybe even more vivid. I was back in that empty deserted landscape but now I was walking in bare feet and I could feel the dirt under my feet and see the little puffs of dust that came up as I walked, and there was a smell. It's... it's hard to explain, but it was a bit like the smell you get around the smith's workshop when they are working, maybe sharpening steels. You know that smell, sort of metallic and sweet at the same time. It was the smell of blood, of course. I smelt it afterwards, when I was at the temple of Kali in Calcutta and they were killing goats, that same sweet/metal smell, except in the dream I couldn't see where it was coming from, and there was the eye up there in that brownish looking sky. It was still closed, or more or less closed, but you could tell by the way the muscles moved near the lid that it was going to open. Or maybe it was trying to open as if there was a hell of an effort involved. Well, that was it for me. Good casting or no, I took that bloody figurine and I went out on the aft deck near the rollers. We were alongside the C platform in East field but where I was standing was the blind side. Facing me was just that empty bit of sea north of Cochin East and I took that bloody thing and threw it over the arse end into the ocean. I half expected something to happen when it hit the water but it just sank out of sight with a bit of a splash.

There were no dreams that night, leastwise none I can remember. I slept well on the ship for the first time in months, then at around twenty three hundred – I'd just come back on watch to do the handover – well, it was just then that the call came in from C platform. We'd pulled off and been steaming away for six hours or so by then. That was the first we heard of that fire, but of course you all know what the score was later. Flames three hundred feet into the air, no fucking lifeboats, not even a standby boat on site.

We were the nearest rescue crew, and by then we were eighty bloody miles off. That job was right up there along with the Alpha and the Deep Water Horizon, two hundred casualties, and no survivors from her crew. We reckoned from what we found when we were clearing up afterwards, that some of them went into the water to get away from the fire. But there were tiger sharks in that area so I don't expect that they were in the water for long.

Was there a link? I don't know is the honest truth. That's the thing about all that stuff, you know? There's no certainty. There's just belief, and, for me at least, that just doesn't cut it. But I don't think I'll be chanting Shiva's name for hours on end to find out for sure, just in case. You understand?

CHAPTER ELEVEN

Back on the ferry, Andy's call to engineering was bearing fruit. Down in the tank top void space where only the rats and the occasional marine surveyor ever ventured, George Chang, the ferry's third engineer, was trying to account for the odd increases in the water depth in the bilges that Andy had reported from the bridge. He was the most junior officer of the San Fong's engineering crew, one step up the ladder from a greaser. He had enough training in marine propulsion to hold a ticket, but he was still inexperienced enough to be mistaken that being detailed every low level job that came along was a vote of confidence in his abilities.

George was the youngest son of a Chinese family and a major disappointment to his father. The elder Chang was a stern traditionalist who believed that it was a son's destiny to carry on the family business, the family name, and the elder bloodline. George, infected from the start of his life with Western notions of independence, had other ideas.

His independent streak, manifest from the very early years of his schooling, was not an acceptable characteristic to his immediate family. His mother loved him dearly, and unconditionally. He was, after all, an only and much longed for son, born after three daughters who would bring nothing to the family but a favourable marriage at best. But George's unwillingness to follow his father's wishes for his career grated constantly on the elder Chang.

Even then he might have eventually found an acceptable outlet for his restless spirit, if it had not been for a chance encounter. At seventeen he had found the adolescent urgings of his sexual drives were too urgent to ignore. He experimented with Western pornography but his mother's shock at discovering centrefolds under his mattress simply confirmed his certainty that the real thing was a mystery that he must explore, quite literally, in the flesh. He began to slip out of the house, late in the evening, while the elder members of the family slept the sleep of the just.

There were a fine selection of bars in Miri and most of them doubled up as 'happy houses', as the Chinese community called them, where, for a few dollars, a succession of willing young girls introduced him to the mysteries of sex.

On one morning, in the early hours, while the sun was dragging itself up out of the ocean in a puddle of reds and oranges, he had fallen into conversation with a much older man, a sailor of forty years and more experience, and an unlikely friendship between the two, begun in the waiting room of a cheap brothel, had blossomed.

Jimmy Henson, the sailor, was a simian-looking little Scot and he had a thousand stories to tell. His second hand experiences opened up, by proxy, a whole new world for the impressionable younger man. George, for the first time, found that he had an aim in life. He searched about for a qualification that might bring him closer to seagoing, and found one, in the courses advertised at the Marine School in Singapore.

For his part George's father was satisfied, now that his errant son was finally prepared to apply for a university level course and to stop his endless, aimless, drifting. The old man saw nothing beyond a university degree level qualification. For the time being, it was of no importance that the Marine certification course would lead, three years down the line, to a career at sea. For the first time in his life, George applied his excellent brain to something more than hedonism.

Three years later, with a third engineer's ticket and an endorsement in diesel propulsion, he had achieved his wish. The day he graduated, the old man was satisfied only in that his son was to be an engineer, a skilled and honourable profession and a welcome change in status. George had worn a rented gown and a stiff mortar board with a golden tassel that was hired from Ede and Ravenscroft like every graduate the world over.

When it was done, after the obligatory photograph of him grasping his rolled Certificate of Competence, he had taken the next step, and three days later, without a word to anyone in his family, he had turned up at the seaman's office in Miri. From there the trip to the ferry and his first seagoing berth was no more than a few minutes walk.

His parents didn't realise, even then, that the son of the family had left them to go to sea. By the time the truth came out, the ferry was already a hundred miles out in the China Sea and he had signed ship's articles and was beyond recall. Such was the start of George Chang's life as a sailor and by the night of the typhoon he was, at least in his own imagination, already a seasoned hand.

It was with the overconfidence of inexperienced youth that he opened the steel hatch that led down into the dark spaces below the lower deck plating. A set of iron rungs led down into the murk. It was dark down there, dark and smelly, with a rich mix of spent diesel, lubricating oil, and filthy stagnant water. Three feet below the open panel in the floor he could see his own face reflected in the water surface, looking back at him as if from a dark mirror. Water in the bilges is hardly unexpected on a ship, but the level of the seepage was far greater than George had anticipated. To the right of the hatch, submerged in the water, he knew there were intakes for the electric bilge pumps. They were big rectangular grills at the mouth of a duct around forty centimetres square and the mouth of each intake was covered with a checker pattern of heavy wire mesh to protect the inner workings of the pump from ingested debris.

Right away George saw a chance of real personal kudos in the situation. If he were to lower himself into that dark, wet, smelly space and clear that grid of the debris he could see from above, thus freeing off the pump and allowing it to void the water overboard, he could finally show the rest of the crew that he was as good as any of them. Filled with the overconfidence of inexperience, flushed already with the anticipated warm glow of approval from his seniors, he lowered himself through the inspection hatch, gripped the uppermost rung of the access ladder and let himself fall into the water below.

The water in the bilge was usually only a foot deep, but it had by that stage reached a depth of five feet. The pump intake grills were consequently sunk deep in the murk. At that stage George had no real concept of the danger he was in. He took a deep breath and ducked under the surface, blindly reaching for the intake grill. He knew that the corners of the grill were held by simple turnbuckles and the grill itself was hinged at the top edge. In theory all that was needed was to slip the grill free, and lift it on its hinges, thus clearing the duct. With that done, all it would take to start the pump would be a hard push on the reset button that was by then only a few centimetres above the surface, bright red against the white paint of the bulkhead. George slipped the turnbuckles by feel, tasting the foul water in his mouth. His lungs were bursting with the need for air. Finally he surfaced, gasping and spluttering dirty water. He could barely see. The lighting down there was weak at the best of times, and the few bulbs that were still working were sunk in dirty water so that they gave only a feeble glow in a halo around each covered globe in its watertight housing.

Eventually his eyesight cleared enough to resolve the reset button. It was no more than a foot from where he stood. Impulsively, not considering the consequences, thinking only of his glorious vision of himself as the hero of the hour, he pushed the red plastic button marked 'reset'. Down below him, in the dark, five hundred horse power of electric centrifugal pumps kicked into life.

At first, he thought that something had grabbed him from below the surface. It was as if a giant hand had grasped him round the middle and dragged him inexorably towards the intake duct. The steel edges of the duct rammed against his chest, his groin, and his left upper arm, holding him immobile with his mouth and nose a little below the turgid surface. George Chang had just time to realise that, while still aboard the ship, he was going to drown. By the time the blockage that his body had caused had tripped out the pump again and stopped the flow, he was already dead. Freed by the falling back pressure, he floated belly down in the darkness, unknowing, unaware. Up above, in the control room, his brave efforts went all unnoticed.

Ships like the San Fong, designed as a ferry with a cavernous hangar space in the main body of the hull represent problems for designers. That big empty space, alternately an empty void and a close packed gathering of heavy lumps of metal, can cause major shifts in the ship's stability depending on the loading. In extreme circumstances, even in the relatively mild waters of the English Channel, such ferries, badly ballasted or not adequately sealed against the sea, have been known to lose stability to the point where sudden capsize situations develop. The lessons learned from the Herald of Free Enterprise disaster were well learned. In modern ships the situation is controlled by ballasting, pumping sea water into tanks well down in the ship's hull thus shifting the weight to a more stable balanced position.

San Fong was from an older generation of ferry boats, built in the days before The Herald Of Free Enterprise, when stability considerations were secondary to profit in the list of builder priorities, but, because of her long history as a car carrier, she did have a system of floodable ballast tanks that allowed the bridge crew to flood or pump out the voids below tank top level to add or discharge weight to improve her stability.

Such a ballast system was a good, and long tested method of holding her stable at sea, but it did assume that there would be a degree of control from the bridge. The increasing, and up until then more or less undetected, flooding below decks was outside the control of the ballast system, and, as such, it was no more than a huge weight of sea water that was simply free to move as the ship rolled. Instead of acting as a steadying weight, the free water below decks built up its own kinetic energy, as the waves outside the hull coincided with the natural ebb and flow of the free moving mass within. From there on whatever was to happen was outside human control, obedient only to the blind laws of physics. Disaster was waiting only on the natural frequency of the water sloshing inside the hull matching the period of the waves outside. The end result of this rather abstruse bit of fluid dynamics was that without any obvious warning, as a cross sea slammed hard into the starboard side, the weight of the free moving water inside the hull shifted itself hard against the hull to port.

On the bridge they were still unaware of the problem to come, until the moment that the ship heeled hard over and gave a sickening lurch. The port deck rails were suddenly under water, and the inclinometer swung violently from a scary, but quite acceptable thirty degree list, to an insane, off the scale reading. At the same second, the wail of half a dozen different alarms cut through the air. The starboard screw was lifted clear of the water by the movement, and, deprived of the resistance of the water spun to a revolution limit far outside its makers intentions. The propeller slammed one blade after another into the surface, churning a pool of foam, and the over stressed bearing in the gland, finally strained beyond endurance, cracked and fragmented. The strain on the shaft, alternately free to spin and suddenly checked by hitting the water, was immense.

The gearbox that the prop shaft was attached to had a sacrificial part within its grinding mechanical heart. No more than a single high tensile steel shear pin, it was meant to break in order to protect the engine from catastrophic damage in case the propeller suddenly met resistance. Years before, and half a world away it had been replaced. The replacement pin was just a fraction too strong. There was a dreadful grinding crunch like a locomotive running itself onto a coral reef and the starboard reduction gear stripped. At the same moment, the starboard engine suddenly found itself running without load and, already throttled up to the limit to cope with the storm conditions, the engine cut out and stopped. As it happened, the antiquated power generation system on the ferry, tying the main electrical power supply to the starboard engine meant that losing the starboard engine meant losing mains electrics as well. For a heart stopping moment, the engine room, the bridge, the passenger decks, the whole ship, were plunged into pitch dark, before the emergency gennie cut in and produced a dim half light throughout the ship.

Andy Fitzroy came back to awareness to find himself half lying against the bulkhead that had once been the left hand wall of the bridge deck. There was a cut on his scalp somewhere and, as head wounds will, it was pouring blood that flowed down his face in a sticky flood. At first he thought that he was blind in the right eye but it was just blood, and a quick wipe with the back of one hand restored his vision to twenty/twenty again.

Andy was a seaman through and through and, like most men who have spent a lifetime at sea, he recognised the situation for what it was in moments. Like any good skipper, he was very near a part of the ship he commanded, and he knew, without any need to consider, that the ship was mortally damaged. From the very first, he knew full well that this situation could only result in one end. Now there was only the relentless logic of survival to deal with. The ship was already as good as lost, the passengers and the crew were his only concern now.

In the water, on such a night, unprotected human beings would have very little chance. There remained only a slim hope of rescue. In the radio room directly off the bridge, Jim Chen, the on shift radio operator, was in a similar state to Andy himself. The violent lurch had thrown him hard against the grey painted steel cabinet of the side band transmission gear. He was conscious, but only just. While the skin of his scalp was intact, he was still in a state of muddy half consciousness. Just at that moment, Jim was not really aware of where he was. He was young for a sparky, just twenty three, and his operator's license was so new that the San Fong was his first trip out as radio officer. He was vaguely excited by the emergency, more excited, in fact, than he was frightened by ship's sudden hideous list. Inexperience cushioned him to some extent from the realities of the situation. The shouted commands seemed to come from far away, as if it no longer concerned him.

Andy shouted across the little radio room. "Put out a full mayday right now, Sparks. Give our position as far you can," he said. "Don't wait for a response. Make sure the IMO beacon is active and for Christ's sake, get that mayday out quickly, Mister. We've no bloody time left."

Stunned and confused Jim Chen might be, but the mention of a mayday touched a deep-rooted reflex that was beyond the need for thought. He grabbed the mic, halting its wild swing at the end of its coiled wire, switched the radio to channel sixteen with a quick practised flick, and started to make the call that every sparky dreads.

"Mayday, mayday, mayday," he said into the mic. "This is inter-island ferry San Fong, we are disabled and listing in heavy seas. All ships in the vicinity please render assistance as soon as possible. Our IMO beacon number is K Kilo, R Romeo, two, niner, six. I repeat Kilo Romeo two niner six. All ships receiving please respond."

The speaker above the desk crackled with idiot static until Jim realised that he still had the mic keyed to transmit, effectively blocking incoming traffic. The second he released the key, the call came in.

The voice on the speaker was calm and measured, as if this were a routine call. It said, "San Fong, San Fong, San Fong This is Salvage Tug Typhoon Star. San Fong, I have a fix on your beacon and we are about two hours steaming from your current position. We are willing and able to offer immediate assistance, sir."

Jim keyed his mic again, responding to that miraculous offer of help. "Typhoon Star, Typhoon Star, this is San Fong. Our present situation is that the ship is listing thirty degrees or so, and we have only auxiliary power. If the situation does not resolve we may have to instruct abandon. Can you recover survivors from the life boats in that situation?"

The Star's operator came back on channel, measured and laconic as ever. "San Fong, Typhoon Star, that's affirmative, sir. We have a rescue zone and will rig scrambling nets ready before we reach your position. How many persons are you?"

Jim was in the routine now. "Typhoon Star, we have two hundred plus passengers and thirty four crew. Total of two hundred and thirty four souls aboard. I copy your scrambling nets. I will keep you updated as the situation develops. If we abandon there will be a maximum of twenty, I repeat, two zero Watercraft fully enclosed life boats, plus thirty or so float off survival rafts and three Whittaker capsules."

"Copy that, San Fong, Typhoon Star listening out on channel nineteen. One niner."

Then there was the click of a closed transmission. Jim took up the microphone one last time. "Nineteen, copy that Star, San Fong, listening out."

Jim switched the radio to nineteen, a less used channel than the international hailing channel sixteen that would allow him to talk direct to the tug without competing transmissions to interfere with the traffic. That done, he called through the open radio room door.

"We have a rescue ship on the way, captain. He's a salvage tug. He says he's eighty miles or so off and is making all speed to our position. That's the only answer to our mayday so far, sir. Do you want me to try to raise anyone else?"

Andy thought for a moment. Comms are important in emergencies, and he needed the radio man right where he was. It was best that he had something to occupy him while he waited. It meant that there was less time for him to think. "Roger that, Sparks. See if you can raise anyone else a bit nearer to us, and keep me informed, Mister."

"Sir." Jim twirled switches and Andy heard him start again. "All ships, all ships. This is a mayday call from inter-island ferry

San Fong. We are disabled and possibly sinking. Any one who can render assistance, please respond. For location purposes our IMO beacon is number Kilo Romeo two niner six."

There was a short pause before Jim began again. "All ships, all ships…" but the only response was smooth, meaningless static.

CHAPTER TWELVE

Down below, on C deck, Sue Fangsu was awakened from a fitful sleep by the sudden shift in the ship's orientation. She was wedged into a narrow bunk and pressed against the bulkhead by her sleeping companion, a hefty Chinese who had picked her up ten minutes into the trip, while the ferry was still trundling down the river out of Miri. Sue had no especial intention of working aboard the ferry when she joined the ship, but the fact was, that there was a chance of the relative privacy and comfort of a cabin below decks, instead of trying to sleep in the open corridor where the ship's stewards were constantly disturbing sleepers as they went about their duties.

It was nothing that she hadn't done a thousand times, and for a lot less gain, and it was honestly just one more client who saw her as a willing piece of meat to be bought and paid for. For her, it was just one more time to shut her eyes and go away to that private spot inside her head that no one else had ever, or would ever, touch. Set against the discomfort of the corridor, and its dusty smelling threadbare carpet, letting herself be used just one more time was nothing…

The Chinese man next to her mumbled and stirred a little. Presently he farted. For a few moments she thought he might wake, but he had a fair load of rough rice wine on board before his fumbling efforts to rouse her to something other than submission that night. As far as Sue was concerned that was a lost cause from the start, submission was what he had paid for, and submission was all he was going to get. Ten minutes after his grunting sweaty climax, he was asleep and the ferry's sudden lurch and violent change of orientation had failed to waken him.

Sue was a whore to be sure, but that accident of birth did not make her stupid by any standards. She knew, from the first moment, that no ship that lurching like that was a good place to be.

She struggled her rather ungainly way across the narrow berth, straddling the fat bulk of the Chinese to slip over the edge of the bunk to the floor. The cabin was at an angle, even though, this far down into the hull, the angle was less severe than it was on the bridge deck. The slope was against her and it meant that climbing out of the bunk was effectively climbing up hill.

Her clothes were scattered on the cabin floor, where she had dropped them, and she pulled herself into a semblance of normality, hauling on nylon panties and a bra and topping the whole lot off with a satin mini dress. It was not an outfit to face the elements in.

Looking around, she noticed the fat man's coat, folded roughly across a chair and she quickly slipped it on. Beside the bunk, on the side table, she saw his wallet. It was fat with Indonesian banknotes, and, if there was ever a time that she needed cash to start a new life, this was it. Twenty seconds afterwards, with the wallet safely stashed, she was ready to go.

It was as she reached the heavy cabin door that she realised that there was a problem. The ship, in her violent lurch, had twisted a little, not enough to disturb the naked eye, right angles still seemed right, but the twist in the ship's structure was enough to warp the door frame. Try she might, even using all her strength, the cabin door was stuck fast. A lesser woman might have simply given way to panic, but years of living on her wits had honed Sue's survival reflexes to the nth degree.

At her feet, at the bottom of the door, there was a square panel let into the door panel itself, called a 'catflap' by sailors the world over. It was there against just such an eventuality as this. It was a hangover from the days of the murderous convoys of World War Two, when thousands of merchant sailors had died, many of them trapped below decks by just such warped cabin doors.

One solid kick to the escape panel would pop it from the door, and leave a narrow but useable exit route to the corridor. One good solid kick did, indeed, do the job. Sue had the common sense, even then, to turn her back to the door and kick with her heel rather than her vulnerable toes.

The way to the corridor, and the open deck, was suddenly open. Crawling on her hands and knees through the escape panel, she was suddenly aware that the carpet in the narrow corridor was squelchy and wet, oozing dirty water between her fingers as she put her weight on it.

The corridor itself was like a scene out of some classical version of hell. The emergency lighting was deep red, reducing everything to shades of blood and blackness, with very little tonality to give any detail to the picture. Still, the escape route signs were bright and clear, glowing with their own ghostly light, showing the way out. Taking a deep breath, and mentally squaring up to the situation, Sue started on her way up to the open deck.

CHAPTER THIRTEEN

Up-grading the 'pan pan' call to a full mayday had remarkable little direct impact aboard the Typhoon Star. There were no klaxons blaring the emergency, no screaming sirens, and no red lights. Outwardly, the only effect was a radio cabin pipe over the ship's PA system informing all hands that the Star was now the only responding vessel to a full mayday call with an ETA on the site of the incident, some two hours hence.

On the Star the little gathering in the control room consisted mainly of specialists among the crew and, of that group, only Zac the medic had an actual role at this stage, and that was a simply preparatory one. Shipwrecks, as they all knew from previous bitter experience, produced a mixed profile of casualties unique to themselves, and different from any other kind of disaster.

There were always the near drowning cases of course, those poor souls whose immersion in cold water had been long enough to allow them to swallow and inhale a fair amount of sea water. They were the sleepers among casualties, the ones who while they were outwardly normal when they were first recovered had hidden secondary symptoms that would only show hours after exposure.

Then there were those who were suffering from simple cold exposure, whose core body temperature had been reduced to a lower than survivable level. For them, rewarming was the definitive treatment, though even that required great care, if they were to survive, and Zac carefully laid out the filmy metallised insulating blankets ready to hand. Those, at least, were sure to be needed. As for the rest, that great group of mixed casualties, that covered all those from the survivors suffering from fuel oil poisoning, all the way to those with massive bleeding, the only useful preparation was to be ready for anything. They were the group of casualties who would always be the real challenge in every emergency.

Zac, having left the others still gathered below, took himself up three decks to the ship's infirmary. It was far too small to be called a hospital, but there were three adjustable beds bolted to the deck to stop movement, all fitted with drip stands for giving sets and railed off to keep casualties in place. Examination lights were slung from the ceiling above two of them. The room was lined on two sides with cupboards and lockers, one of them as painted bright red with the warning notice 'Controlled drugs, are you sure you are authorised to dispense?' painted on it in stark black.

Zac went meticulously about his preparations, setting up a giving set with saline for each bed, breaking the seal on the thick polythene containers, and attaching a long plastic tube tipped with a sheathed wide bore IV needle.

Those drips had a limited life once the seal was breached. If circumstances dictated that they weren't used within ten hours, they would be deep sixed as no longer sterile. From past experience, Zac had little doubt that they would be used. He marked each one with the time in black magic marker, then he took a last look around his little domain and, satisfied that there was no more to be done, he carefully locked the hospital door behind him, and swaying a little to the ship's movement, he made his way back down the stairways to the dive control deck.

CHAPTER FOURTEEN

Not everyone on the crew had an immediate role in emergency preparations at that stage. Steve Anderson, officially Rescue Coordinator, was one of those whose only function at that stage was to wait. When the rescue was actually in progress, it was Steve's job to coordinate messages from the two fast rescue inflatables to the ship, and to control the flow of casualties from the deck, where they would be landed, directing the flow to either the reception area, where the walking wounded would be given hot drinks and clothing, or to Zac's triage unit, a deck below, where the more serious medical interventions would happen.

Steve was ex-grey funnel line and the ingrained discipline that Royal Navy training implied made him superb at his job. He was unflappable, coolly efficient. He was a perfect rescue coordinator, but not a man given to fanciful musings. All of these things made the remaining gathering below decks listen even more carefully than usual when he spoke up.

"I was just a kid," he said. "I joined as a cadet, then sailed as a boy sailor. You know how you are at that age. Ready to do anything that sets you apart from the herd. So when they asked for volunteers to go down to the Pacific and, how did they put it? I think it was to 'observe a British nuclear test'…"

Steve – the rescue coordinator

Christ, lads! What kid could turn that down? We were tasked to take this fleet of old ships down to the test site. I was serving on a destroyer then, newest of the bloody lot she was, the only bloody ship out of the whole fleet that was fit for sea. Later, a long time after we left the UK, when we were well out to sea, a whole lot of other escort ships joined us. Four of them were Australian Navy, I remember, but most of the ships in that little convoy were old flatirons from the wartime lend/lease deal. They were as rusty as fuck, and belching dirty smoke out of their stacks. Honestly, you could have seen them from miles off, let alone the engine noise they were making. They all sounded as if they'd never seen an engineer in years nor a can of oil, or a greaser neither.

What we was supposed to do was to line out these old wrecks at varying distances from the blast. I remember there were two newer destroyers in the fleet, they were late World War Two types, you understand? Well, they were packed with ordnance, you know the magazines were full, like they would be if they were on active service.

I guess the idea was to see if the bomb would propagate the explosion of their magazines. I personally never got to see that bomb. I never went ashore on the atoll, but it looked a pretty enough place from the sea. Those that did go ashore, well, they said that the bomb itself was in a corrugated iron shack affair on top of a tower that looked like an electricity pylon. We laid off eight miles clear. The boffins in charge reckoned it was safe enough at that range (or so they said), and on the day of the blast we sat out on the aft deck in the early morning sun. We was told to face away from the island and sit cross-legged on the deck, with our hands held over our eyes. The idea was that, after we heard the bomb go, we were to stand up, uncover our eyes, and see whatever was there to see.

It was a bloody lovely morning, bright sun, blue sky, a few little flecks of white in the water and perfect visibility. Anyhow we were sitting there and there was this countdown over the tannoy, just like on the films. He starts from ten, and counted back. I can still hear his voice, and the instructions. Ten… nine… cover your eyes NOW… seven, six, five, four, three… BRACE BRACE BRACE, one and detonation.

Now I don't know what we expected, we were all just sitting there and it wasn't till afterwards I realised I was holding my breath. Then it happened, the flash I mean, I saw all the bones in my hands, closed eyelids or no. I had this ring that a girl from home had given me, I could see it around the outlines of the bone of my finger, clear as day. After a second comes this sound, it was like someone rolling a bloody great rock down a stone channel, a sort of deep rumbling that went on and on. Right after that, the blast wave arrives, it was warm, like the wind you feel if the breeze blows over a hot engine that's been working hard for hours. It was like the oxygen had all gone and all you get when you breathe in is this empty hot wind. Anyhow that voice comes over the PA again. "Get up and turn round now," he says, and we all shuffled about and stood. It was harder than you'd expect to get up on your feet, 'cause by then the ship was moving about a bit as the first waves reached us.

First thing we saw was the cloud. It wasn't a mushroom, not right then, just a big fat ball of flame roiling and rising as it rose up from what was left of the atoll. As it rose into the air, it started to spread out. There was every colour you could think of in that cloud, reds and blacks and yellows and blues, and round it, in a bloody great smoke ring, there was a ring of pure white, like ordinary smoke but really thick. And all the time there was this rumbling, like thunder, but louder. It went on and on like it would never stop, and then the mushroom rose on into the sky. We were the best part of eight miles off, I remember, and it still looked close enough to touch. As it got to full height, the top of the cloud started to spread out, like. I heard afterwards it does that when it reaches up to the edge of the atmosphere where the air gets thin and, after a few moments, there was the mushroom, fully formed.

We were all shocked, I admit, not just me. As I said, I was just a kid. But the grown men too. The big hairy arsed matelots were just as shit scared as I was. One of them, he was a big old stoker who must have been coming to the end of his twenty five year hitch, he had tears in his eyes.

We laid off out to sea for twelve hours or so and the cloud gradually broke up. So, by the time we started to steam in closer to gather samples and look at the effects, it was sunset, and in the western sky was the most gorgeous sunset you ever saw.

First thing we came to were the position of the ships that had been moored maybe two miles off the atoll. Among them were the old warships that had been loaded with a full magazine to see what would happen. The first of them was just simply gone, all that was left was the cylinder mooring buoy she'd been tied to. That buoy was clean, like it had been sandblasted, all the paint and antifouling was gone. There was just bare metal with a really fine dusting of rust like a car body that has been through a fire. The second of those warships was still afloat, just, but it looked as if the forward magazine had exploded. All her decks were forced upwards like the petals of a flower, the forward gun turret was just simply gone, all three hundred tonnes of it. Nothing left but the traversing ring where the guns had been. We didn't go aboard her, no one did, our scientists were keen to get samples for the fall out, but, even from a few yards off, the bloody meters were going off the scale.

The deckhouses and superstructure was like the buoy had been. All along one side of the ship, the side that had faced the blast, I guess, there no paint left on her. There was just bare steel plate, as if it had just come out of the shipyard. She was lower than she should have been in the water, so I guess she was taking on water somewhere below decks, but no one went aboard to check. Later they got one of our escort group to sink her with gunfire.

While we were there, gawping at the wreck, the first bird came along. It was a big bird with white feathers and a big wingspan. It might have been an albatross, who knew one bird from another? Anyhow, it came sweeping in and flew smack into our bridge windows. It didn't check in its flight, it just went smack into the glass. It left a sort of ghost of itself in a dusty outline. We must have all heard the noise it made when it hit, sort of a cross between a splat and a thump. It fell dead to the deck not forty feet from where I was working, and, curious, like, I went to look. When I got close, I realised what had happened. Its eyes were… well, they were cloudy, like an old man with really bad cataracts. You know the sort of thing you see sometimes in Africa? All cloudy and bluish white. Anyhow, I could see it was blind, and we picked up maybe another twenty corpses of birds while we were in the area, all of them blind. We couldn't stay there too long because of the radiation of course. The scientists bagged all the dead birds up, all that we could gather. They put them in big black plastic sacks with yellow radiation warnings on. I remember thinking, if the bloody corpses of a few birds are too dangerous to handle, what the hell are we doing here?

So that was Mosaic, the biggest British above ground test ever carried out. The bomb, as it turned out, was near on three times more powerful than they had expected. For a few weeks we worried that something might happen to us. I say 'we', I mean, we didn't talk about it, but I tell you, I was bloody worried. Every time I felt a bit off, I thought I might be dying.

Once, I got a dose of the shits, and I'm thinking, that's it, I'm gone, but the weeks passed and nothing really happened. The MO took a few blood samples for a month or two, but I never heard of any results. Anyhow that, we thought is it, a nuke. Big fucking deal.

Three years ago I met one the guys I'd sailed with on that job. He must have been fifty five or so but you know he looked bloody eighty. Leukaemia, they said, cancer of the blood. Turns out that it's twenty times more common among test vets. I have tests every now and then, and so far all's well, but I tell you what, lads, they were right when they said never volunteer, you never know what you might be getting into.

CHAPTER FIFTEEN

In the cabin so recently vacated by Sue Fangsu, the fat Chinese client, who was named Gerry Ho, was still sleeping, though he was showing signs of stirring. Mr Ho was, or rather had been, an important businessman in the Hong Kong Chinese community and had the distinction of being the 'Red Pole', or enforcer for the local chapter of the Wo Hop Wo triad, a criminal organisation whose origins went all the way back to the eighteenth century.

Gerry Ho had first been introduced to the triad's mysteries by his great uncle, who owed Gerry's father a favour, and sought, by this means, to settle accounts in the least expensive way possible. From the first he was captivated by the ritualised structure of the Wo Hop Wo society. As an eighteen year old he had first entered the secret underground temple of Guan Yu hidden away under the apartment block in Hong Kong. The island was still under British rule in those days.

He had passed under the arch of swords held by senior members of the triad. The arch was symbolic of the initiates' entrance to the triad society itself. Gerry watched fascinated, as the 'Mountain Master', the local head of the order, had struck off the head of a cockerel with his heavy blade and poured the gushing blood into a chalice. There, it was mixed with rice wine, and tasted by each of the seven initiates in turn, before, with the salty warm taste still in their mouths, they had knelt before the Mountain Master himself to take the thirty six oaths of triad membership. In his other life, the Mountain Master was a respectable merchant banker in the colony.

As each initiate intoned the ritual oaths in turn, they knelt before the Red Pole, in charge of discipline, who was in full robes and holding a long glittering executioner's sword. The enforcer struck each man lightly on the neck with the flat side of the sword. As he touched the blade to the exposed nape, the Red Pole intoned the ritual question.

"Which is harder?" he asked. "The blade or your neck?"

And each initiate in turn answered, "My neck."

That done, each man signed a parchment copy of the oaths in his own blood and the parchment was then burned on the altar of Guan Yu signifying that the oath was irrevocable and would bring the new triad member nothing but good fortune as long as he upheld his responsibilities to his brothers in the Triad.

As '49ers', newly initiated members, the youths undertook the routine business of collecting monies due, intimidating those who required persuasion, and defending Wo Hop Wo influence from other triad groups using such violence as the situation required.

Gerry Ho proved himself an apt pupil. He rose rapidly through the ranks, becoming first a 'Straw Sandal', whose number in the triad was 432 and then, as time went by, he rose to become a Red Pole in his own right. As the enforcer, who was responsible for discipline within his branch of Wo Hop Wo, he proved ruthlessly efficient, and given to making clear statements in his business dealings by ordering his assistants, the soldiers among the 49ers, to employ the traditional hatchet to complete their contract killings. Under Gerry Ho there was to be no doubt as to who had taken revenge on the triad's opponents. A killing, of itself was not enough to satisfy his sense of honour, a signal must be sent out to the wider community. That wider community quickly got the message; under Wo Hop Wo rule, within their area, there was peace.

Then came the end of British rule in Hong Kong. Chris Patten, the last governor, dressed in a comic opera uniform, saluted the union flag as it was lowered for the last time on Hong Kong island and the red flag of the People's Republic was raised in its place. As 'Britannia' steamed out of the harbour, past the new territories, 'The East is Red' echoed over the most capitalist society on earth.

While the British had effectively tolerated the triads as a means of maintaining the appearance of law, the communists had long been implacable enemies of the Heaven and Earth societies. Under the rule of Mao Tse Tsung, the triads had been effectively destroyed in mainland China. Now that same ruthless suppression came to Hong Kong.

Mr Ho, as ever, was capable of reading the way the wind blows. He left Hong Kong for Singapore, taking with him only a suitcase of illicit currency and his triad connections. It was, on paper, a sensible move. But a few months after he arrived in Singapore, he discovered that, under the gentle paternalistic dictatorship of Lee Kwan Yu, Singapore was no more tolerant of triad internecine warfare than the communists had been. Besides, his presence threatened to upset the balance between the indigenous Ghee Hi Kongsi and the Salakau triad societies who were already in place. Bloodshed on the streets was not the Singapore way. Mr Ho was warned off, and given three days to leave the island for pastures new.

He sought fresh opportunities, casting about, before finally settling in Indonesia where the history of the triads was less deep rooted but the rule of law was more relaxed.

Mr Ho quickly established a flourishing business running pseudo Ephedrine into the country from the People's Republic's burgeoning pharma industry, and converting it, via an illicit lab in Jakarta, to MDMA to feed the Australian market for ecstasy. It was while he was returning from a deal for those precursors that required his personal attendance, that he found himself on the San Fong that night. He was a long way from the willowy youth who had joined the Wo Hop Wo triad all those years before. He was millions of dollars richer and seven stone heavier.

Ten minutes after Sue Fangsu left his bed, he woke to find himself cold, naked, hungover, half asleep, and completely disoriented.

The light was wrong. That was his first waking thought. The cabin's lighting on the old ferry was by creaking old florescent tubes discreetly tucked away behind frosted plastic panels in the ceiling. Now both of those panels were dark. Instead of the dingy, half yellow glow, there was a blood red light. It looked like the kind of glow that might cascade out through the mouth of the gates of Hell. Also, there was a strange tilt to the floor, the cabin suddenly canted to one side. Worse than that, there was a smell in the air, a foetid mix of fuel oil and wet. Mr Ho was no sailor, but that smell – as any member of the salvage crew on the Typhoon Star could have told him – was the olfactory signature of a ship that was dying. Something in his memories reacted to that smell. He was suddenly very much sober and awake. He realised in bare seconds that the girl was gone, and in moments more, he realised that she had absconded with the wallet that he had carelessly left on the bunk side locker top.

Neither the absence of the girl nor the loss of his wallet really troubled him. Using the company of itinerant whores was a high risk pleasure, even aboard a ship, and he had seen this same scenario a dozen times before. The wallet didn't bother him then, but, more importantly, the suitcase, the battered old leather luggage bag that was full of currency, and MDMA was still where he had left it. He supposed that it was too bulky for her to shift easily. Gerry Ho hauled himself out of the bunk, waited a few seconds while the whirling sensation in his head steadied and then he crossed the few steps across the floor to the case to check it. The latches were still closed, the locks intact. He drew a deep of sigh of relief. The goods were safe, everything else was secondary.

He struggled into his clothes, hauling them on from the heap on the chair that was the cabin's only other furniture. It was only then that he noticed that there was a square void in the cabin door. It was less obvious than it might have been because the light in the corridor outside the door was the same dim, blood colour as the lighting in his cabin, but once he had seen it, that square hole in the cabin door said 'disaster' as clearly as anything inanimate might.

He tried the door latch and turned it. Of course it shifted as smoothly as ever, but that was all, the door, jammed into its twisted frame, was immovable. For a few seconds he stood there frantically hauling on the reluctant door, then he hammered on it with his fists. The door was built to take day to day abuse, structured out of heavy duty plastic and thin steel sheets, It was un-moved by this assault.

It was only then that the first thin trickle of water edged its way over the lower lip of the escape hatch and formed a little rivulet on the cabin floor turning the dark green knobbly carpet a deep brownish, muddy colour. In the corridor outside the cabin, the water was already eight inches deep.

Mr Ho stood there for a moment, looking at that trickle of moisture, unable to take it in. Even in the uncertain light he could see the particles of dirt and dust that the moisture had lifted out of the carpet… and, looking at that trickle, Mr Ho knew that he was looking at his own approaching death.

As an enforcer, a Red Pole, and even more in his early days as a lowly 49er, a foot soldier of the triad, Mr Ho had seen death maybe a hundred times. He had in fact, seen death in many vile and painful forms that he had either inflicted himself, or ordered inflicted by others. But that was always death applied to someone else, a lesser being, a traitor maybe, or a soldier of another triad, or maybe a shopkeeper who had been foolish enough to question the triad's iron rule. Up until that moment he had been certain, as only the extremely egotistical are, of his own inviolability. Always he had been certain that death was something that applied to others. Now it was suddenly irrevocably personal.

And now there was nowhere to hide.

The moments of panic lasted only for the time it might take to take a deep breath. Then the old, cold blooded survivor inside him, the inner man who had risen steadily through the triad structure, cut in and took over.

There was no question in his mind that the ship was in trouble. Staying with her was to court disaster, the cabin door was immovable, the little room was a death trap, the only route was the escape panel.

Standard escape panels according to international maritime organisation specification must be twenty four inches or greater in square section, and capable of being detached from the door they are built into with a single hard blow. The cabin door, having been built in Clydebank, where the IMO regs are taken seriously, lived up to the regulation to the letter.

Sadly Mr Ho, who tipped the scales at twenty two stone, and who was short of breath to the point where simply kneeling on the floor was a great effort, and standing back up again was likely to cause a brief spell of dizziness, did not even come close to the regulation size.

With his head and shoulders through into the corridor and a closer view of the rising water than he would have wanted, his generously rounded middle scraped over the edge of the escape hatch… and stuck fast. For two minutes or so he couldn't believe that this ridiculous situation had happened, But his belly was stuck fast and no matter how far he pulled and pushed the rolls of fat around, his flabby middle simply would not shift.

He struggled until the edge of the escape hatch first abraded his gut then ripped the soft skin in a ladder of shallow bleeding cuts that stung as the dirt ground into them. Even so, even the leakage of blood couldn't lubricate the skin enough to allow him to slip through to safety. He had nothing to grab outside in the corridor to pull against. There was only the carpet and the rising scum of dirt floating on top of the water.

Within minutes the water level had reached the lower lip of the escape hatch three inches or so below his mouth. For the first time in his life, since the time that he had nearly drowned as a young child, Gerry Ho felt the bitter metallic taste of panic rising inside him. The ship gave a groan and the angle of list increased suddenly with a sick-feeling lurch. The water level that had been creeping up, now rose in a rush. His margin of free air was suddenly halved. He was trapped with his mouth at water level and his nose only slightly clear, and then only if he craned his neck backwards.

Mr Ho whooped out his last few breaths, took a deep lungful of the air that was rapidly becoming out of reach, and screamed. It was a high pitched yell, almost girlish, not a sound that he would have ever before thought of in connection with himself, but it was the last conscious sound he ever made.

The old ship gave another of those convulsive lurches and the rising water enveloped him with a rush. His very last impression was of shimmering bubbles as his last breath escaped him and vented to the unseeing, uncaring air of the corridor above him.

The air was just twenty centimetres away and forever out of reach.

Floating behind him in the cabin, in an old leather suitcase, was five point three million dollars in mixed currency and eight kilos of high grade methamphetamine powder. It really didn't matter anymore. Death changes your perspective on the important things in life.

Two decks above the level where Mr Ho was busy dying, Andy made a final decision. As master, that was the radio call that he hoped never to have to make, but, also as master, he recognised the inevitable where he saw it. He crossed the few feet to the radio room door, struggling a little against the list and said, "Sparks, put out a formal mayday right now, if you would. Give our position as far as you are able and activate the emergency beacon. I'm issuing the formal abandon order as from now. After the mayday goes out, you may leave your post and go to your boat station. Good luck to you, Mister."

The words felt like ashes in his mouth. It was a stiff and

formal form of words that had legal significance. From here on inter-island ferry San Fong was officially a derelict, fair game for salvage for whoever could get a line onto her, and her passengers and crew were no longer his responsibility once they had left in the boats. From here on they were at the mercy of the ocean and whoever might be prepared or foolhardy enough to attempt a rescue.

The formal mayday call was made from the San Fong at 00.45 hrs that night. The storm was just passing its peak at the ferry's location, the eye of the typhoon was more or less past her, and the trailing edge of the whirling vortex was drawing clear.

Like many typhoons, this one was extraordinarily disciplined in form. She was a tight whirling circle of foul weather that covered maybe a hundred miles of open ocean. By the time the mayday went out, the worst of the weather was starting to abate. Even so, given waves at thirty five feet and force nine gusts, that night was not one to take lightly.

CHAPTER SIXTEEN

At 00.45 hrs that night, the Typhoon Star's radio shack was its usual oasis of calm, the duty sparks was listening out on channel nineteen, aware that a call from the ferry might come in at any time. Even for an operator with twenty years' experience in the salvage game, that final 'mayday', when it finally came, still raised a frisson of nervous reaction every time

A declared mayday is a blessing and a curse in salvage. It means open season, a prize for the taking if all goes well, but it also means that somewhere out there in the night and the storm, fellow seafarers are fighting for their lives, maybe dying, even as the call came in.

In its way it was a spur to action. There is a tradition on salvage boats aimed at involving the whole crew from skipper to steward in the rescue. Typhoon Star's sparky switched the PA mic to 'open channel' so that he would be heard right through the ship and said, "All hands please be aware, casualty vessel San Fong has up graded their status to a full mayday call. ETA is now ninety minutes or so off. All section heads to stations immediately, please. All other hands prepare for rescue and recovery operations."

Out on the aft deck, where the weather was still soaking the open space with greenish water every few minutes, Taff Jennings was busy. The RIBs, the semi-rigid inflatables that used their glass fibre hulls and bulky balloon floats to brave the very worst that the sea could do, were ready, though in such seas as this launch was going to be a problem. Normally an RIB is launched by a simple crane lift cradle that lowers the little boat into the sea, and in most circumstances this is a well tested procedure, but, on such a night, the only possible way to get the little RIB into the water was to use the lee of the Typhoon Star's hull to defend against the worst of the weather. The lee was little enough protection, but the RIB's, overpowered beyond their modest size, packed a hell of a punch. Twin outboards delivered three hundred shaft horse power to the business end. That allowed them to power over the ocean, skimming their way over the surface, often as much airborne as floating, slipping over the surface and avoiding the worst of the turbulence that would sink a lesser vessel.

The aft deck was lit up but only by the work lights that covered most of the ship. At the very start, Taff used the deck radio on his belt to call the bridge to ask for the floodlights to be switched on. A few seconds afterwards the deck was as bright as a summer day. The big arcs cast a halo around the ship and showed an area of sea that looked deep, dirty green where the light penetrated, and nearly black where it didn't.

Out in such a sea, Taff knew very well what the chances were for a survivor with no more than the flimsy protection of a life jacket. The ruthless maths of survival time had been calculated with exquisite cold precision using helpless concentration camp victims during World War Two. An RFD lifejacket will keep you afloat, alive or dead, for hours on end but smashing waves would make taking a breath near impossible, spray hood or no. Every desperate gasp risked a lungful of water and a couple of those would be more than enough to settle matters.

Billy Cheung, his number two cox, a Singaporean national with nearly as much sea time as Taff himself, joined him, swaying across the deck and using whatever came to hand to steady his progress.

"Bad night, boss," he said with the normal understatement of the weather adopted by professional seafarers. It was if acknowledging the weather might make it worse.

Taff nodded and leaned closer, to speak into Billy's ear to defeat the scream of the wind. "It's going to be a bugger of a job picking up survivors in this."

"If they survive, boss," said Billy.

Taff nodded again. They were both thinking the same thing. Tonight would more likely be a time for body bags than for Zac's attentions in the hospital. The water might be relatively warm but the wave motion was cruel. The water was in violent chaos, simply breathing in such conditions would be a struggle.

Down below, Steve Williamson, the camp boss, or chief catering officer, was making his own preparations for the impending rescue. First order of business was a full urn of chai, that over-powerful, naval blend of hot chocolate and sugar that had traditionally rewarmed immersion cases since the days of the Atlantic convoys and the Wolfpacks.

Royal Navy mythology aside, it did have a good solid hit of life enhancing sugar to provide a quick energy burst, and its air of nursery comfort was, at least in Steve's opinion, as good as anything from the medical stores that Zac could provide. Steve came from a much older tradition of seafaring.

The next job on his list was less homely, but equally important, in its way. Typhoon Star had three walk in freezers, as well as two cold rooms, normally used for vegetables and fruit. Steve went to the second and larger cold store, fixing the hook and eye fastening to hold the heavy door against the wave movement as he went. Then he methodically moved the contents across to the other store. It was mainly fresh veg, and, as they were between supply runs, there wasn't that much to move. He wanted the cold store empty before they started on the rescue, on such a night he was sure that it wouldn't stay empty for long.

CHAPTER SEVENTEEN

Evacuation at sea is rarely the ordered and disciplined movement of humanity of the training drills. On the San Fong, emergency preparations at the start of the trip, at least as far as the passengers were concerned, extended to nothing more than a brief exhortation in English, Cantonese and Tagalog to read the Safety Information posted on the inside of every cabin door. That was combined with an announcement that the ship would be leaving in ten minutes. For the sake of passenger morale there was deliberately no sense of urgency about the announcement, prefaced as it was by the inevitable and reassuring "in the highly unlikely event of an emergency", spiel that accompanies all such public notices. The net result was that even those passengers who understood the tannoy had paid it very little heed. When Andy Fitzroy finally made the decision that the risks of abandonment were lower than the risks of staying with a sinking vessel, there was already a degree of panic among the passengers. The flooding below decks was getting worse, and even the most inexperienced among those aboard could feel that awful dead-in-the-water roll as the ship, ballasted beyond its safe level by the flooding, began to wallow rather than riding the seas. Even before any formal decision. By the time that Andy made that last announcement, there was already a drift towards the hatchways to the open deck.

Little clusters of humanity were gathered at the exits. Not wanting to be trapped below, there was a simple human need not to be confined below while the waters rose. Meanwhile, crew members, already clearly disoriented and confused – safety drills were not a high priority in the South China Sea – went about preparations that they only half understood.

In theory, each lifeboat has an assigned coxswain who trained, again in theory, to handle the little vessel and to take it through the launching drill. In theory the coxswain's job on a lifeboat is straightforward. On a well found ship it might be. San Fong was a sad example of the old axiom regarding preparation and performance. Typical of the problems that night was the sad story of lifeboat number six, a totally enclosed Whittaker Capsule powered by a single diesel engine and davit launched from the port side of the ferry. The Whittaker's odd shape and flying saucer style appearance had given it the nickname of the 'Smartie'. It looked and behaved in an eccentric fashion in the water, though it was, to be fair, very near impossible to sink, unless it was subject to tremendous structural damage. That given its odd shape made it hard to set and keep any kind of a course. The cox of number six boat, supposedly in charge, was an eighteen year old seaman called Liwei Wong. His seagoing experience, before he joined the crew was mainly pottering about on clinker built fishing boats with not a great deal in the way of power and nothing in way of safety gear.

Liwei's reaction to the abandon order was like that of a rabbit caught in approaching headlights. He heard the click that the PA always made before any announcement over the open channel. He knew the ship was taking on water and realised that the list signified real damage but in his limited experience on fishing boats that leaked all day and every day, simply shipping water was an annoyance rather than a danger. How far he was wrong in that comforting belief was brought home to him very rapidly. Andy's voice on the PA was the same unruffled laconic accent that he always used but this time the message was far from routine.

"This is the captain," came the flat voice. "Would everyone please pay close attention to the following message. This ship is now in serious danger of sinking and remaining aboard her is likely to prove very dangerous. All of you must now proceed to your boat stations. Do NOT go out onto the open deck until the crew tell you to. Do NOT attempt to board a lifeboat until you are instructed to by a member of the crew. Gather at your muster stations now please. Proceed in an orderly fashion. Do not run. There is no immediate danger. Leave your personal belongings in your cabin. Do not attempt to take luggage with you. You will not be allowed to take your luggage into the lifeboat. Thank you and good luck to you all."

Then in a more formal tone altogether he went on.

"This is a crew message for all designated crewmen with emergency duties. Code is Abandon Abandon Abandon, and may God protect you all."

Liwei reacted with a mixture of fear and anticipation. Just for a second he saw himself lauded in the local media, accepting the grateful praise of the people he had saved. For some reason all of them, at least in his mind's eye, were young, female, and universally lovely. The glorious vision lasted just long enough to get him out of the accommodation area and onto the deck outside the heavy steel door that led to the enclosed space below decks. The journey to number six boat was less than twenty metres, but it more than made up in violence for the limited distance. Inside the ship the wind was a howling background sound that went on and on. In the open it was like a living thing that tried to throw him over the rail into the greeny black hell that lurked just outside the deck lighting. His first step into the open space resulted in him being thrown hard into a steel railing provided as a handhold to steady passengers as they crossed the deck. The impact broke one of his ribs on the left side and left him gasping for breath until the immediate agony subsided a little. All thought of rescuing nubile lovelies vanished in that lightning bolt of pain.

Struggling to hold onto his breath, he pushed himself against the wind and found that by doubling over until he was almost in the position of an ancient hag in a fairy tale, he could shuffle forwards a little and make progress. The international rescue orange of the Whittaker's hull was looming in the murk and, through the driving spray and rain he could see that the hull of the little boat was beaded with rivulets of flowing moisture.

There was a lull in the wind, a brief few seconds as the air gathered itself for another onslaught. He took the chance to move and then he was there. The plastic shell of the capsule was varnished and his face resting against the hull itself, he could see the tiny imperfections in the gel coat that made up the boat's structure. Then, like a blessed mirage, he saw the black lever with the big red arrows pointing to it and with the lovely word 'open', stencilled on it.

The lever shifted easily and the hatchway fell open in front of him.

Liwei half fell through the open hatch, helped on his way by another violent gust and he landed hard against the housing of the Lister diesel engine that drove the boat. The impact made the pain in his side flare up for a few moments before it subsided to a deep hot ache. A chance gust took the hatch and slammed it shut.

With the worst of the wind and rain shut out, he was sheltered from a direct assault by the weather. He lay there for a few seconds before hauling himself upright. Capsules like boat number six were designed to hold thirty survivors and allow for one man launching.

Training took over. Liwei swayed across to the rudimentary control panel holding his hurt ribs, and flicked the cabin lights into life. For a mercy they came on instantly showing that the battery was at least partially charged, and sparing him the need to pump the air starter up to pressure. The circular interior cabin flickered into solidity around him, though the lighting was by a little bulb in a wire cage that glowed pale yellow and cast deep shadows so that the effect was like a railway station waiting room at four in a winter's morning.

His command position was more or less in the centre of the little boat with a small glazed conning tower above his head, that stuck up from the top of the curved hull like a tiny gun turret. In front of the cox's seating position, where he would be held in place in a hard plastic seat by a hefty five point nylon harness, was the panel for the diesel and, extending from the davit directly above was the steel launching cable. All he needed now was the passengers.

Outside the boat on the deck of the ferry, matters had deteriorated, even in the time that it took Liwei to make it to the capsule. All semblance of order was long gone. A frantic mass of struggling humanity was trying to get through the hatches to the boat deck. They were held back by those people in front whose first encounter with the weather outside as they faced the open deck gave them cause for thought.

An old Chinese gentleman, raised in a culture where deference to age was axiomatic, edged forwards into the clot of bodies, serenely confident in the certainty that no one would willingly hurt him or impede his progress.

The crowd, now far beyond such niceties and intent only on survival, simply rolled over him. His last conscious thought, or rather emotion, was that of disbelief as they crushed the life out of him, and left his body, no more substantial than a bird's might have been, lying broken across the iron hatch combing in the opening.

Out on the deck number six boat was nearest to the companion way, the little capsule seemed like an offer of hope in a desperate situation, so around thirty people massed in a body towards it, like moths drawn to the fatal beauty of the candle flame. Number six boat had an access hatch some four feet wide by three high. The first arrival slammed it open and the effect of three men trying to force their way through it at one time was simply to clog the entrance solidly while the crush behind them prevented anyone from moving back to ease the pressure.

A wave came out of the dark, a crossing sea whipped up by a

chance combination of wind and water. It reared up above the deck rail forming for a brief moment a green/black background to the bright orange Smartie, then it broke in a solid mass of foamy water, and of the thirty struggling survivors, suddenly only six were left. The rest were simply gone, leaving not a trace, not a bloodstain, not even a last cry against the suddenness of their ending. They were first simply there and then were simply gone, torn from the periphery of the group by the sheer weight of water.

The backwash foamed through the hatch of number six boat as three hundred tonnes of cold water tried to return to the ocean at one go. It triggered the pumps in the Whittaker's bilges that threw the water overboard almost as fast as it had come.

The remains of the group, those left in the deck hatchway, waiting to make a run for the capsule, saw the clear space that had miraculously opened in front of them. Taking their chances they ran across the deck, bent by the wind, slipping even on the green non-slip surface, stumbling to the lighted hatch of the capsule. Single survivors came one after the other, three men, a woman and two children, the small remnants of the group that had tried to cross the deck.

Liwei had a rapid decision to make. By the book he should stay at his post, order those people he already had aboard to strap in and wait while others joined them, but the deck outside the hatch was deeply awash already. He could see the muster area where the crowd had gathered, and it was empty but for the windswept and sodden slight figure of Sue Fangsu emerging from her nightmare climb through the battered and lurching labyrinth of the accommodation decks. True to her relentlessly tough upbringing, Sue took a quick look at the sea to judge her chances and rushed across the space like a hare breaking cover in a summer evening meadow.

She fell through the hatch and lay gasping on the dirty decking of the capsule. Liwei looked outside one last time to measure the risks. Under his feet he could feel the capsule floating on the flood, tethered only by the steel launch cable. To Liwei's credit he was willing to make a decision. He had his survivors, granted far fewer than he would have wished, fewer than the manual said that he should have, but no one else was in sight. Liwei decided it was enough. He slammed the hatch closed and dogged it fast against the weather then, seating himself at the con he hit the electric start while he offered a brief unspoken prayer to whatever gods govern survival that there would indeed be enough life in the old battery. There was a quick heart stopping, moment when it seemed that the diesel was not going to fire and then it kicked into rattling life. The immediate effect was a foul cloud of burnt diesel that filled the little cabin, but the engine was at least running. With the capsule awash Liwei had to judge his moment to launch so that it would fall into the water rather than smashing against the ship. Finally, in a brief lull, he saw his chance and hauled on the release lever.

There was that awful 'stomach rising to the back of your throat' moment, as the Smartie fell free, meeting the water thirty feet below with a muffled thump and casting her hoisting eyebolt free as the davit line fell slack. The screw bit into the water and the craft was under way and at the mercy of the ocean.

CHAPTER EIGHTEEN

First was the whirligig motion that affects all Whittaker capsules in the hands of an inexperienced cox. In training, the way that the capsule spins in the water is amusing, an occasion for gently mocking a fellow course member, or perhaps an occasion for the victim to stand a round of drinks that evening. Out here, in the middle of a violent storm, the effect was anything but amusing. Liwei swore in ripe Cantonese, cursing himself, cursing his passengers, cursing God and the ocean, an Asiatic version of the Flying Dutchman. Finally he got enough of a grip on the realities to take action and he shoved the tiller first to one side then the other, finally reaching a position where the lifeboat seemed to be making progress away from the threatening bulk of the ship. He glanced out through the porthole in the conning tower, seeing the ship's side through a stainless steel mesh that protected the glass.

The iron cliff of the ferry was receding rapidly, though he could not tell if the increase in sea room was due to his helmsman-ship or the sea. Whatever the reason, life boat six was on her own in a raging sea.

As number six boat disappeared into the flying scud, her

successful launch was marked by very few aboard the ferry. Many of the passengers – those who were instinctively fearful of the ocean – were still below decks where the emergency lights and residual warmth gave an illusion of safety, protected as they were from the wind and weather. These were the 'non survivors' according to the ruthless logic of the survival psychologists who study such things.

They were those people who, in the event, find themselves unable to think or act for themselves. Most of them, in the fullness of time would be trapped within that illusory comfort while the water rose to take them.

Most of the ferry's crewmen were not affected by that dangerous complacency, but even so there were those who clung to the illusion of safety that the ship still gave.

Not numbered among those, Harry Chang was a sea man with half a century of experience that encompassed among other things, a session as a greaser on a British merchantmen. This was not even his first shipwreck. He had been on a tanker that had been lost when she broke her back in heavy seas, another victim of the design fault that had begun with the British bulk carrier Derbyshire. That time Harry had been on the forward end of the ship at the very moment when the heavy aft unit parted company and went down like a brick before his eyes. Harry had no illusions about the vulnerability of ships. In his experience, the sea always had the final say in such matters. He was methodical in his preparations.

Harry shared a cabin on C deck with his oppos and the first move he made, long before the situation became desperate, was to pick up a small watertight package from his cabin. It was well wrapped with silver grey duct tape filched from the engine room stores. Enclosed in that package were three thousand American dollars and his seaman's book and passport. With that secured, Harry took a bright yellow survival suit from his locker and hauled it on. Survival suits were a luxury not offered to passengers on grounds of expense. In fact few of the crewmen had access to one, but Harry Chang had stolen the suit from a previous assignment, squeezing it into the bottom of his kit bag under a stack of old boiler suits and fake Levis from the market in Shanghai to camouflage his larceny.

There was no foresight in that theft, aside from the regular foresight of the professional sailor that assumes that the sea will always do the unexpected. Now the survival suit, watertight and with built-in boots and hood, offered a small chance of making some attempt at braving the water outside.

He stashed the duct tape wrapped package neatly inside the suit, and pulled the plastic zip fastener tight under his chin. Personal preparations complete, he took himself off to the boat deck, using emergency routes that avoided the main passenger areas of the ship. Most of them were by way of vertical ladders consisting of nothing more than iron rungs welded to the steel plating of the bulkheads in a vertical line.

As he reached the head of the final ladderway, lifting a steel hatch to give him access to the boat deck, a wave flooded across the horizontal surface above him and crashed down towards the lower decks in a cascade that washed over him like a waterfall, nearly knocking him off the rather precarious hold he had on the ladderway.

The flow of water over the deck took the hatch out of his grip and slammed it open against the plating. Taking advantage of a brief lull, Harry hauled himself through the opening and emerged into a nightmare world of flowing water that was rushing across the deck and out through the freeing ports and thus overboard.

Harry was battered and beaten by the water but he was protected from the worst of the flow as far as wet was concerned by the tough neoprene suit. Wearing it, he remained warm and comparatively dry. Number four boat was nearest to him as he emerged from the hatch and, for a blessing, there were two other crewmen near to the launching station. They looked very young, both dressed in crewman's overalls and both soaked to the skin, with their hair plastered into streaks down their faces.

Harry was officially assigned to number one lifeboat but to attempt to reach that boat, positioned as it was on the opposite side of the ferry, and to the windward as well, was suicidal on such a night. The two deckhands, one of whom he recognised as a steward from the galley on A deck, would be a poor launch crew, but, under the circumstances, they would have to do.

Number four boat was a Watercraft. It was an old fashioned, totally enclosed lifeboat that had originally been painted a smart international rescue orange, but was now a washed out pink with many years of exposure to the elements. Unlike the Whittaker capsule, the Watercraft, while still totally enclosed in a thick fibreglass canopy looked like a conventional lifeboat. The Watercraft was launched from two davits, gantry like structures that were used to lower the boat over the side via a complex of steel cables and ratchets.

In theory the process was simple. A large counterweighted lever simply eases the tension on the cables and the weight of the boat hauls it over the side and simultaneously lowers the hull into a position where the hatchways are aligned with the deck for boarding. This process ideally needs power to the electrics, and if that motor fails or that power is not available any longer, there is a simple steel ratchet handle that does the same job, albeit with a good deal of manual effort. Harry took the situation in at a glance. Power launch was simply not going to happen with the generators out of action. Instead he set his impromptu helpers to wind the boat out by hand.

As it happened, the lifeboat davits were one of the few bits of the ferry that had been subject to a genuine servicing schedule, at least as far as regular painting was concerned. As a result, the ratchet lever that drove the manual launch system was solidly encrusted with a thick layer of marine grade paint. The one characteristic of that particular coating is that it is undeniably tough. It took the combined efforts of both of the deckhands, and a bit of hammering with a heavy lump of discarded scrap iron that lay in the lee shadow of the lifeboat, to shift it. The result was jerky and juddering, not the smooth progress that the makers had intended, but, with a few minutes of desperate hauling, the Watercraft hung ready in the launch position.

She swayed on the cables as the ferry shifted with the seas. The lifeboat's hatches opened at deck level next to a simple steelwork boarding platform on the ferry, ready for such survivors as might be there to board. The platform that bridged the deck of the ferry to the lifeboat hatch was made of perforated checker plate, intended to allow excess water to drain, and it gave a direct straight down view to a boiling ocean thirty feet directly below.

No sooner was the lifeboat in position than the doorway to the accommodation deck opened to disgorge a disparate crowd of desperate humanity. They were a mixture of bewildered passengers who had no idea where to go next, and a sprinkling of the San Fong's crew, some in overalls, some in steward's whites, who had finally decided that the 'every man for himself' principle applied at that point.

Harry did the best he could to load them into the lifeboat. It was crowded and smelly with the stink of burned oil and salt water mixed with the acrid reek of terrorised sweat. It is a mixture that engenders panic, in even the most well-trained and level-headed, acting directly on the primitive levels of the brain, but Harry cajoled and swore, taking no excuses, simply ordering the survivors into their places in the boat.

A youngish man with bright wide eyes that showed far too much of the whites hesitated at the crossing into the lifeboat, looking down directly into the sea below, but only as long as it took Harry to grab him by the shirt and haul him into the hatch. It was a rough system but it worked. In the end forty people were crowded into the lifeboat. They were wet, they were bleeding in a few cases, all of them were shivering with shock and fear. The whole group showed the over-bright eyes with black shadows under the eye sockets, of victims of disaster throughout the world. Harry directed them as best he could, showing them how to strap themselves in with the nylon lap belts, and trying as far as was possible, to reassure them. That was not simply altruism on his part. People in a panic could easily unbalance the little boat and though she was totally enclosed, and self-righting in theory, he had no wish to try out the self-righting system in practice.

By that point the ferry was head down in the water, dragged

off balance by the increasing weight of water below decks. The sharp point of her bows was dipping ever more deeply into the oncoming seas, and each time she dipped, she came back a little more slowly as the load below inexorably increased as she flooded.

Soon, Harry knew full well, there would be one dip too many, as the ship passed the point of no return, and began her slow slide towards the seabed. At that point, as the launch angles became more severe, there would be no chance of getting the little lifeboat clear.

Harry slammed and dogged the hatch shut, finally closing the boat off from the world outside, and silently sending a final goodbye to those left on the ferry. The screaming wind died, shut outside by the hatch and the huddled survivors were left with the smell of diesel oil in the semi-darkness.

"Chen," Harry shouted to the crewman nearest the launch wire, "get that brake off, will you? It's past time we were gone."

Chen was a steward. He was tall for a Chinese but he had the build of a padded skeleton and pinched, ratty, features. He had, once, been shown how to launch a lifeboat. The brake wire which hung beside his seat reached through a gasketed hole in the roof of the life boat connecting directly to a simple lever on the davits above. A tug on the wire lifted a brake shoe on one end of a simple lever that operated against the action of a counterweight. Once the brake was released it left the boat free to fall under gravity.

Chen took a good grip on the wire and hauled down hard against the weight. It took a solid tug. The counterweight weighed something like three kilos of iron. The lifeboat weighed two tonnes dead weight and the extra mass of the passengers took that to nearer three. It accelerated rapidly towards the water, trailing the launch wire as it went.

Harry did not realise what had happened until after the event. From the moment the boat hit the water's surface, the sea was already giving him more than enough to think about. The hull hit the water with a smack and a padded impact that shook everyone inside it to the bone.

Harry vaguely registered someone screaming, a high womanish scream, but there were passengers aboard after all, and he had other things to worry about.

He started the diesel, and, by more good luck than good maintenance, it fired first time. The ship was to the port side of the lifeboat, a threatening iron cliff, that towered over them, and, tough though it was, if the boat was thrown against it by the sea it might well be smashed like a fibre glass egg. He threw the helm hard starboard, felt the screw bite, and suddenly the boat was a live thing under his hands as she swept away from the wreck and floated free into the storm.

CHAPTER NINETEEN

Typhoon Star was equipped with the best radar technology that money could buy, as well as location equipment able to track the beacon that IMO regs require of all sea going vessels. The San Fong did have an IMO beacon but, at her last port visit, an over enthusiastic electrical fitter had managed to partially sever the lead that connected the beacon to its aerial. As a result the signal was erratic, slipping in and out of visibility and giving the impression that the casualty was underwater long before the event.

On the bridge, Jamie Piper, the watch officer who was technically in charge of the rescue, regarded the erratic signal with some distaste. He was a graduate of the Trinity House Maritime School in Hull and the Merchant Navy officer training course, a professional seafarer through and through, but perhaps a little young, as yet, maybe too ready to accept the sad reality, that, simply because regulations said that something should be so, it would be so.

For the last hour or so the radio messages from the casualty, the one certain way of being sure that she was still afloat, had become less frequent, less organised, and more frantic. In the end the ferry's operator had left his set locked to 'transmit' on an open microphone, effectively sending an endless stream of static. A random voice for listeners to home in on.

Jamie was fairly certain that, given the weather and the situation, the chances of effective salvage were slim to non-existent, but he was young, and willing to regard the saving of the casualty crew as more important than a simple salvors' fee. The Star's owners, safe on land in distant Singapore, might well have thought otherwise.

John Williams, who happened to be the Star's helmsman at that stage in the rescue, was very near Jamie's polar opposite. He was coming up to retirement after fifty years seafaring, having started as a deckhand trainee, a 'deckie learner' on the distant water trawling fleet. His skills were hard won. He was not paper qualified, and he was inclined to treat the Star's young mate with a degree of, not suspicion exactly, but certainly with a degree of reservation.

Jamie for his part knew this full well and, though he knew he had no business in the world trying to prove himself to the older man, he still felt vaguely inferior when it came to practical seamanship.

"A vile bloody night, John," he said. "What are their chances in this, do you think?"

"Fair to fuck all, I would say," said John, "especially if they are in the oggen. Have you ever been in the water yourself? By accident, I mean?"

For a moment Jamie felt that he was being subtly tested but he dismissed that as paranoia and said, "No, thank God. Well, in training of course on the CBOS unit, you know?"

CBOS, the Combined Basic Offshore Survival course, was thought of with some contempt by seafarers who regarded it as a short cut allowing non-mariners to pretend that they understood the sea.

"Right," said John, and blew out a breath as the crossing waves tried to haul the ship out of his control. He eased the starboard throttle back a notch and gave a soft grunt of satisfaction as the Star obediently answered the helm and came back onto her course.

"There was one time…" he said, shaking his head as if he was trying to clear the memory and rolling a smoke with the one-handed dextrous familiarity of long practice. "A long way from here it was, up in the Arctic grounds. Cold water up there, see, fucking cold. Only three degrees or so with brash ice half the time…"

John – the helmsman

I were a deckhand then. It was on the old Vandal. She were lost off Bear Island ten years after I was on her, just vanished with all hands. There were no beacons then, of course. If you didn't check in then, the ship just bloody vanished as far as the outside world was concerned, and of course some skippers used that as a way of hiding their position. Competitive, you see? Out there you are nothing but a hunter gatherer. Only so much fucking fish in the sea and no prizes for helping the opposition. Well, the Vandal, she were a stern freezer. Big ramp down the arse end to haul the bag up and slippery as hell it was during cold weather. I were sent to free a snag. Happened more often than you expect, you know? You'll be pulling a full bag and suddenly the warps come tight. They were fifty tonnes breaking strain those warp lines, built to stand up to the ship pulling the net through the water, and they were made of braided steel, like a crane wire. Anyhow, this night they were tight like bloody bowstrings and the whole issue, net and all, were caught up on the lower part of the ramp. Bloody dangerous situation that. If a warp should break, god help the poor bastard that gets clipped by the free end. When it happens, it whips like a flying chainsaw. Anyhow, more often than not, the snag is on the ramp itself, and if you keep pulling with the winches at full belt you can tear the net like paper.

If that happens a full bag of fish goes right to the bottom and takes fifty thousand quid's worth of gear with it. What happened that time was that the starboard otter board had caught on the lip of the ramp. Now when you are fishing, the otter board sort of flies through the water and hauls the mouth of the net open.

They are bloody big things on a ship that size, like fucking garage doors made of oak planking and with steel edges and riveted up to shape. It were the rivets that had caused the problem, never see that nowadays, of course. It would be all welded construction now, and that leaves nothing to get caught up. But she were an old ship, the first of the stern freezers and her gear were even older.

Anyhow there we were – we could tell by the strain gauges that there were a good bag of fish on and there it was, damn near close enough to touch, and just hanging there, with the odd seabird chancing its arm to pick up a stray fish where it was sticking out through the mesh of the net.

Well, the mate, he says to me to go down the ramp with a safety line on a harness and free that bugger off. They started by easing the tension on those winches. The idea was to pull the bag back aboard real slowly while I was supposed to ease the edge of the otter board over the lip of the ramp with a long crowbar as it came. We reckoned that once it started to slip over the edge of the ramp, it would slide from there on.

I went down the ramp and they kept the tension up on that safety line as I went. It was clipped to a canvas harness and that made it hard to move. I saw the warps start to ease back off as the mate reversed the winches a bit, and after a few seconds, the leading edge of that otter board popped off the edge of the ramp and slipped back into the sea. So all the tension was off it. As soon as it were clear I called to the mate to haul away easy, and the warps started moving again inch by inch, this time going gently inboard, and I could see the leading edge of that bloody otter board, just under the surface. I got the point of the crowbar about where I thought it would be right and got ready to lever the thing inboard. It came a lot easier than I expected. One minute it was underwater and the next it was beside me, edge on and upright with its narrow edge resting on the steel of the ramp.

Now you have to remember that the bloody otter board is a big lump of kit. Fucking thing weighs maybe two tonnes. If it had toppled I'd not be telling you the story now. As it happened it stayed upright, sliding along on its edge 'til it was well past where

I was standing there on the ramp but as it went, the steel strip on the edge of the board caught that safety line and sliced it like a bloody knife.

The waves were breaking of course and with nothing to hold me I was standing on a sloping ramp that was slippery as fuck with the water and slime draining from that net. I sort of felt myself start to slip towards the end of the ramp and I was in the bloody water five seconds after.

They tell you what cold water immersion does and I've heard the theory, but it doesn't prepare you for that bloody cold. I were only wearing overalls and a sweater and I was wet right though right away. I remember thinking that I was near to the fucking screws. I got this picture in my head of those big bronze blades cutting me to bits, then it was as if the water went solid and suddenly I'd got something to hold onto. It was the bag of course, and there I was, hanging onto that fucking trawl net for dear life. I was maybe twenty foot from the Cod End but the lads hauling the bag couldn't see me from where they were driving the winch and the next thing I know I'm hanging next to twenty tonne of dead and dying fish right over the hopper.

In one way I were lucky. The lad standing by to cut the lacing to empty the net sees me in time and hollered to lower the bag a little so he could get me off. It were only after I was back on the deck that I realised how close I'd come.

The thing is, lad, every time we go to haul some poor fucker out of the water, I think what it's like and in my head I'm hanging there again clinging onto that net with the hopper underneath me and shivering like a bloody leaf in a high wind.

CHAPTER TWENTY

In number four lifeboat, the caged bulb was a meagre thirty watt filament lamp, yellow and dim. Under those lighting conditions, fresh blood looks nearly black. Chen, the young steward who had trapped four fingers on his left hand in the launch wire was not screaming any longer as shock took over and endorphins flooded his bloodstream. He was holding his mutilated left hand in his right and trying to stem the bleeding from the severed stumps.

Harry was still far too engaged in trying to keep the boat more or less upright and away from the wreck of the San Fong to concern himself with the needs of his passengers. The lifeboat was driven by a single four bladed propeller enclosed in a steel cage that was designed to protect casualties in the water from the whirring blades as they were turned by a three litre Lister Petter diesel. It was a tough and reliable system that had evolved over thirty years of design whose inspirations stretched back to the Second World War. Even so, the weather conditions that night were nearing the design limits for the lifeboat.

Harry had very limited visibility from the cox's position. His viewpoint was no more than a narrow rectangle through a sheet of armoured glass maybe twenty centimetres by eight. He could see directly ahead, and a little to the side in a restricted cone, but, essentially his whole world view at that point was confined to an area of water ripped by massive winds and waves that towered into the air on all sides.

Abruptly the wave motion caught the lifeboat's bows, and swung his viewpoint around to take in the ferry. She was still afloat, but effectively awash, with waves breaking over the open deck and only the bridge tower still relatively dry. It was obvious at a glance that anyone still below decks was beyond help. On the aft section of the deck, above the old fashioned sweep of the fan tail stern, a few survivors were still gathered in a forlorn little knot.

All of them were wearing standard issue life belts, the international rescue orange jackets bright points of colour in a whole world that was coloured in grey and green and white.

There was no way of trying to reach them. To take the fragile fibreglass hull of the lifeboat close in to the wreck would be to invite disaster. Harry had no real choices. Following his heart, trying to save a few more lives, would in all likelihood simply lose the ones he had already rescued. He turned her head into the weather and that narrow cone of vision swept over the little group on the stern like a searchlight. Then they were gone into the storm as if they had never been.

On the bridge deck of the sinking ferry, Andy was still at his post. This was not the result of some antique idea of the skipper going down with the ship. Andy was a pragmatist. His actions were informed by the realities. Simply, he knew very well that the chances of an unprotected human body surviving in such seas were very nearly nil. He had no longing to die, but, like many old time sailors he was well aware that prolonging the process of his dying and extending his suffering was all that he could achieve by struggling at that point. The bridge windows were half inch thick armoured glass, gasketed with thick rubber that sealed it to the steel frames. The windows were panoramic, extending in an angular curve to both sides and sharply raked inwards to reduce spray. Andy's view from the bridge took in three boats still hanging in their davits unlaunched, but with the seas sweeping the open decks every few seconds there was no way to reach them, let alone get them into the water. Cheung, his number two, was still there beside him, another victim of the wreck who knew very well that there was nowhere left to go. His long brown face was as impassive as always. Still, Andy felt he had to make the gesture.

"By all means try for a boat," he said, "if you think it's worthwhile, Mr Cheung."

Cheung looked at the shrieking nightmare outside the bridge window.

There was not a flicker of emotion there.

He simply shook his head. "No good, Captain,' he said. 'Nothing to do now but die."

"It's been an honour to work with you, Mr Cheung."

"Wei."

Still not a flicker of emotion but Andy could have sworn that there was an edge of humour in the voice.

"Was that a joke, Mister? In the face of death? You are a brave man, Mr Cheung."

"Wei. You too, boss."

Andy said, "When I first went to sea, Mr Cheung, they used to say, the people back home, I mean, that a man who did that had gone to 'follow the sea', as if it was a religion."

Cheung thought a moment and then he said, "You ever see that poem, boss? The one that starts: 'There are no roses on a sailor's grave'?"

As if she had waited for that cue, the old ferry began a deep iron growling from inside the hull, what the old U-boat skippers called 'breaking-up noises'. Deep below decks, where there were only the floating dead to observe the event, the bulkheads were giving way. A great bubble of trapped air, silver against the dirty green of the ocean, came up from below and burst on the surface.

Suddenly the air was heavy with the stink of marine grade fuel oil. The ship gave a lurch, as if she had taken a heavy punch below the water line, and the stern rose at an angle, submerging a little group of survivors on the fore deck. They were instantly scattered by the ocean, reduced to tiny orange dots in the infinity of water. For a few moments they were visible, then, just as quickly, they were gone.

The ship began her final slide to the bottom. A rough scurf of debris, old bits of rope, the odd lump of scrap timber, a stray boat bumper that some one had long ago forgotten to secure, all washed up the deck in a tide of rubbish, moving towards the bridge island. It was like looking through the glass of an aquarium full of dirty water.

For a few moments, the emergency lighting on the deck glowed blood red through the murky green water that had swallowed it. Andy, watching the water rise, knew perfectly well that this was the final stage, that the old ship was very soon going to go on her final dive.

Seconds passed in a slow eternity of waiting, the water reached the foot of the bridge island and began to rise towards the bridge windows. By then Andy was holding onto the chrome rail of the engine control panel to keep his feet against the increasing incline. The water level reached the bridge windows, increasing in speed and depth. He had just time to observe the clear screen, the little spinning disc that was intended to throw water off the bridge windows to give a helmsman a clear view of the sea as ahead of him.

There was nothing to see now but a short cylinder of illuminated water and a ghost image of the bows of the ship, underwater already, and lost to the ocean. Then the rising tide reached the doorway on the bridge wing to his left. The radio room was inundated in seconds, provoking bright electric flashes from the reserve batteries as if someone was taking photographs of the ship's dying moments. The incoming flow swirled around his feet. It was icy cold and bore the iodine scent of the ocean with it. Cheung was gone, swept out of the bridge into the sea by the rushing water. It threw Andy off his feet, disoriented him, threw him against the control panel. His last few moments held nothing but confused images of swirling bubbles and cloudy water. At the very last he saw, or thought he saw, Cheung's long brown face beside him, then the dark came.

In number four boat, Harry saw the old ship first shudder and then take on that bows down attitude that presaged the final plunge to the bottom. He was the only living observer and he saw the last moments through his narrow envelope-sized viewing port. Where the wreck had been, the ocean roiled and shuddered, trapped air and fuel oil belched up from below, marking the spot as a spreading pool of debris, timber, life rings, even a float off raft that had survived the wreck. It all bubbled to the surface. Around the float off raft, loops of white nylon rope hung uselessly, waiting for survivors who would never come. Here and there, floating in their international rescue high vis flotation jackets, were the dead, lolling with the movement of the ocean that lent them a brief illusion of life. Harry looked at the scene with what he thought was impassive detachment. There was no one in that dim little space that by then smelled strongly of fresh blood and vomit, to comment on the tears that flowed down his face, marking the rough stubble with crystal drops that were as saline as the salt water outside, if less threatening.

CHAPTER TWENTY ONE

A quarter of a mile from boat number four, the Whittaker capsule bobbed in the surface turmoil, not holding a course, not even running before the wind, simply floating as a ping pong ball might, bobbing on the surface. The Whittaker, despite its futuristic design, has a dubious reputation among sailors.

Often derided as 'Smartie' because of its saucer shaped hull and orange colour, it does have undoubted advantages. It is a unique concept born out of the realities of emergencies at sea. Real life is far from the orderly training drills where pairs of immaculately trained deck hands launch perfectly maintained life boats from recently serviced davits into a calm sea. The Whittaker is launched from a single point hoist on a single central hoisting wire, it does not need any special training to launch it and because of that unique system it is capable of one man launching at need.

The Whittaker is also very nearly unsinkable, capable of floating on, despite taking massive structural damage, and able to bob along like a lightweight UFO on the worst of seas. Given its advantages, you might think that it would be universally adopted, but the Whittaker has a flaw. Round boats, from beach toys to monsters like the Whittaker, suffer from the coracle effect.

From the Iron Age onwards, coracles have been used to fish fast flowing rivers and, probably from the very first moment that they took to the water, people found that the little round hull was difficult to control. Lacking a keel allows movement in all directions with equal ease.

Like a coracle, the Whittaker capsule, in the hands of an inexperienced helmsman, will go where it will, spinning like a high tech whirligig beetle on a pond, no matter how much effort the cox puts into moving the stubby steering lever.

The San Fong's Whittaker was launched into a sea that was running in all directions at once. It was carried by the wind, skimming over the surface until the wreck of the ferry itself was just a vague shape, outlined by the emergency lighting as it rose and fell into and out of view as the waves and the wind shifted the relative positions of capsule and wreck.

No one in the life capsule was aware of the final fate of the ferry. In the case of the Whittaker, 'totally enclosed' meant just that. To avoid potential weak spots in the hull the designers built their hull structure very nearly without ports. Inside there was only semi-darkness and the curved wall made from roughly finished glass fibre so that the mesh of the matting showed through the gel coat.

The survivors sat around the periphery of the hull in a circle like a tribe of Amer-Indians in a tepee, smoking a pipe of peace. Each of them was held roughly in place by a sturdy nylon lap belt. The diesel rattled vilely. It had been serviced last around the time of the millennium and the oil levels were barely high enough to protect the crankshaft bearings from seizing. Even if they had been in the mood for conversation, the survivors would have had a hard time making themselves heard above the racket.

Liwei was in no mood to talk anyhow. His ribs hurt from the recent impact and there was a feeling almost as if some delicate tissue was tearing each time he tried to take a deep breath. The passengers were mostly in shock, sitting glumly in their uncomfortable fibreglass seats. Two or three of them had already vomited as the erratic motion got to them. The air inside the capsule was fetid with the stink of human waste and fear. Liwei was beyond caring about any of it. The hurting inside the left side of his chest was getting worse. It felt as if someone were using a razor on his quivering skin to slice into his insides. It was a sharp, thin, pain of extreme intensity. Liwei did the best he could to hold the Smartie steady against the seas, though the Whittaker bucked and kicked like a live thing under his seat. But the view he had of the outside world was growing dimmer. It was strange, as if his field of vision had reduced itself to a small circular patch where the centre of his visual field had been once, upon a more happy time.

Liwei did not know it but the truth was that he was close to dying. The three broken ribs from the earlier impact were oblique fractures, all of them leaving two dagger tips on the broken ends of each bone. With every move that Liwei made, the shattered bones dug deeper into the soft pink meat of his lungs, ripping through the protective layer of the intercostals and exposing the interior of his chest cavity, finally tearing the pink sponge of the lung itself. With each breath that he took – shallow breaths they were now, deep breathing hurt too much – bubbles of free gas leaked out of the tear in his lung and tracked upwards into his chest cavity. Despite the severity of the wound, the leaking gas caused little pain in itself. Instead there was a feeling of uncomfortable fullness, as if he had just eaten an unwisely heavy meal. It was increasingly hard to breathe, and, as the gas tracked upwards, the skin around the base of his neck began to feel uncomfortable. If there had been anyone there to check, they would have felt the characteristic 'rice crispies' feel of crepitus under the skin.

Liwei kept going as long as he was able, fighting the increasing darkness at the edge of his vision that threatened to wash away the reality from around him. Finally it was all too much. He slipped quietly from his cox's seat without any fuss, and hung limp against the five point harness that kept him in place.

Jenny Woo was sitting directly in front of the conning tower of the Whittaker. She was a tall woman for a Chinese and slim to the point of emaciation. She had high strong cheekbones and a sharp, almost delicate facial structure. She was on the San Fong that night because she was on her way to complete the sale of her restaurant business to a national chain. It was the culmination of a lifelong battle to succeed that had seen her build a modest empire from scratch.

Jenny was a classic example of the Chinese belief in the ability of hard work and determination to create a good life from poor beginnings. She had been born to a poor family and her mother was a survivor of the Japanese occupation. Indirectly, the stories she had been told at her mother's knee had influenced Jenny's attitude to society in general. As a child she had learned that, to other races, the Chinese were regarded as subhuman, and women were forever cursed by their gender to be the bottom of the hierarchy. She was, her mother had taught her, destined to be forever alone in the world, trusting only herself, and constantly subject to the plots of those who would harm her. She learned the lesson well.

In truth, Jenny had never been subject to anything more overly racist than the usual casual social contacts, but her mother told her stories of the days when Japanese troops had beheaded Chinese men in the main square with Samurai swords for no better reason than the insane delusion of imagining that they were following the ancient code of the medieval knights. Her mother's stories had given Jenny a profound distrust of strangers, and in business, as she gradually built the restaurant chain from a pavement café to a plush chain of eateries where Miri's great and good regularly brought clients, she was honest but absolutely ruthless.

Jenny had the odd brush with the local triads, like any business in the Far East. At one point a suave young man with a thin face that looked as if it had been carved from glass walked in one night and told her that her business was now under the protection of the Wo Hop Wo, the price of that protection being eight hundred Singapore dollars a week. It was not really significant as a business cost, but Jenny was determined that she was stronger than the social circumstances that had allowed this foolish young man to threaten all she had built. More than anything else it was his air of entitlement to walk into her life and threaten her that drove her on to react as she did.

Sitting in the small back office with its walls covered in clips of invoices and order sheets, sitting in the everyday clutter of a small business, her mother's stories and warnings were suddenly made flesh on the other side of the desk. She heard him out and then suggested that he send someone more senior to discuss matters. Even that was a calculated insult, and intended as such. To send the man away empty-handed to his superiors was a loss of face that he would find hard to swallow.

In the end she arranged a meeting with the head of the local extortion group, laid on lush food in a private room and gave every impression of willingness to come to an arrangement that would suit both of them. Jenny was no fool at this game. She played the part of the hostess to perfection. She put up a great show of demure interest in all he said and even carried on her air of surprise and solicitude when he clutched his chest and turned purple under his yellow skin tones before falling face first into a dish of crispy duck. She left him there for a few minutes, watching with clinical interest as his feet kicked their last few twitches until she was quite sure he was dead, and then, and only then, composed her features into a grimace of shock and surprise, before she rushed, screaming for help, from the main dining room next door. No one thought to check, but in her left hand pocket was a small empty glass phial that had once held puffer fish venom. Later when she sent a sumptuous funeral gift of jasmine flowers to put on the man's grave, the empty phial was attached to the wreath instead of a signature.

In a way she had thought that murder should be less mundane, or that at least she should feel guilt at the removal of another human being, but Jenny was introspective enough to search her own conscience and find it clear. Death, in the society where she found herself, was a fact of life. The extortion gang had tried to take what was rightfully hers and under the modern trappings of civilisation the realities of dog eat dog were as pronounced as ever.

The local triad were quick to understand the implications, after all such warnings were their stock in trade. One restaurant was not worth disturbing the peace for, especially where its owner was as ruthless as they were, and fully prepared to act in her own defence. For a time, they weighed the good effect that Jenny's assassination might have against the inevitable police interest. The price, they decided, was not worth the problems it might generate. For the time at least, Jenny and her business were allowed to trade in peace. That incident had put steel into her soul and given her a backbone of pure iron. Never ever again would she allow anyone to victimise her, least of all a man.

Jenny struggled to her feet, staggering with the motion of the deck, and grabbed hold of Liwei's harness to steady herself. One look was enough to conform what she already suspected. Whatever ailed Liwei, he was unconscious, and from the pallor under his brown skin, he was likely to stay that way. The other passengers were screaming at her, yelling in a mix of Cantonese and English for her to leave Liwei be. They were victims of the universal human need to yield authority to expertise, no matter how spurious the basis of that authority might be. Jenny ignored them all. One oldish woman whose iron grey hair was hanging around her face in tattered ringlets was screaming loudly at her in Cantonese, yelling at Jenny to sit down and leave the sailor alone. For a moment it looked as if others might join in, and matters were in doubt, and then Jenny turned to address her directly.

"Shut the fuck up and let me do what's needed," she said in Cantonese and the old woman subsided, shocked into submission by Jenny's response. It was transgressive in a way that few westerners could have understood, because this was a culture that reverences the old. There was one unforeseen effect though. The same need to submit to authority now transferred itself to Jenny herself. Jenny looked around the crowded little cabin. There was no response. They simply sat in a circle like red Indians in a tepee, all eyes and shocked faces. Taking silence for consent,

Jenny moved unsteadily to release Liwei from the harness which still held him upright. At first the nylon straps refused to yield but after she snapped the five point buckle loose, Liwei's limp body collapsed forwards. Jenny paid him no more attention, and hauled him out of the way by main force, using strength she didn't really know she had. Later, if there was to be a later, when the adrenaline wore off, she knew that she would pay her dues to muscle strain. For now she could only feel a godlike certainty that she was doing what was needed. In the meanwhile, Liwei was dying on the deck. His brain starved of oxygen, he felt nothing of importance. The deck of a lifeboat is hard and unyielding and is not, under most circumstances, the most comfortable place to pass over from. The glass fibre hull was cold and Liwei's left ear was jammed up against the housing of the diesel, but at that moment, as the light faded around him, it felt to Liwei as if he were lying on the softest downiest feather quilt in the world. It was like resting on a cloud. Presently a vivid point of light manifested itself in the centre of his vision. It was golden yellow, and it radiated warmth and a feeling of security. Entranced, Liwei drifted gradually towards the light not even questioning this newfound ability to drift through space at will that he had suddenly developed. The storm outside, and the sea, the cramped cabin and the stink of burned diesel oil and human sweat faded away and he found himself quietly transported away. As far as the other survivors in the Whittaker were concerned, Liwei simply died, blood bubbling from his mouth as the last massive bleed carried him off, but for Liwei it was a moment of transcendent wonder before, finally, he was gone…

Jenny, no longer interested in him, took his seat at the con and held the stubby steering arm in her left hand. Sometimes the gods are kind. The sea was pushing the little craft rapidly towards the darker patch in the flying scud that marked the Typhoon Star.

Aboard the Star, at the very moment that Liwei was dying a few hundred metres away, the crew were going through the final preparations to recover survivors from the sea. The eye of the typhoon, that calm central area that covers around three quarters of a mile of open water, was gone. The following wall of the storm, the area when the winds abruptly change direction by a full hundred and eighty degrees had passed over their position. One of the very few mitigating factors that night was the extremely tightly organised nature of the storm. With the eye past, in another few hours the wind would be no more than a full gale, force nine at worst, maybe even eight if things worked to their advantage. The sea would remain turbulent for twenty hours and more yet but the very worst of the storm was past.

Their first indication that they were near the wreck was, as always, the smell of fuel oil on the wind. It is the constant that accompanies every shipwreck. As a vessel sinks, the oil in her fuel tanks rises through the vents that are intended to allow air into the bunkers to stop the engine's constant sucking thirst creating a vacuum and starving them of fuel. There was always that slick on the surface after a wreck, sometimes no more than a shimmer of iridescence on the ocean surface. Sometimes, if the wreck were a tanker say, the escaping oil forms a thick yellow green tide of sludge that forms an unlovely mix called mousse when it makes contact with sea water. They say the oil calms troubled waters by reducing the wave height a bit. Years ago they would pump fuel oil deliberately onto the sea in the hope of giving the lifeboats an easier time. Often, in wartime, when wrecks were common, the spread oil would ignite, either by accident or deliberate malice, and survivors would escape the wreck, only to burn to death in the water, an irony in death that escaped most of them.

There was no fire after the San Fong slipped away and the diesel from her tanks did no more than stain the still turbulent ocean but there was still the smell of oil, always the smell of oil. Taff Jennings stood in the lee of the accommodation block and sniffed at that oil stench as if it were perfume on the neck of a beautiful woman. He was a veteran of more sinkings than he could be certain of remembering with clarity. After a while they merged into one, always that smell, always the search that was frantic at first, growing less urgent with time, for those specks of international rescue orange against the endless, white flecked surface.

There was a drill for such sightings, as there was for everything else. It is all too easy to lose a given point in a space where there are no reference points. In the ocean, standard procedure was to sing out. Once you would simply shout, but nowadays you use a deck radio. At the same time the observer points at that elusive orange dot and keeps pointing. No matter if the wave movement means that the speck of orange vanishes in the wave tops you keep on pointing until the ship grows close enough to allow rescue.

Taff's sighting was not orange but yellow and there was the flicker of a bright xenon strobe ticking its regular pulses into the half light of the after storm morning light to help them find it. He took the deck radio from his belt and said into it, "Bridge, this is Taff. I've a target sighting at three o'clock off the aft deck. Do you copy its position?"

"Roger that, Taff." The bridge crewman could have been talking about anything for all the emotion that came over in his voice. "Copy your target, Taff. We're on it. Billy has his field glasses on it, says it looks like a Smartie. Maybe there might be a bit of salvage in this after all. Could you get the surface jumpers ready in case?"

"Roger that, bridge," said Taff. "Surface jumpers are standing by."

Taff switched channels on his deck radio to eight, the operating channel for the job. He said, "Dive crew, we have a Whittaker capsule visual ten minutes steaming away. Could we have the duty jumper and number two ready on the aft deck station, please."

"Roger that, Taff. On our way."

After a few moments, the hatchway behind him opened and two men both fully dressed in dry suits and wearing ready inflated RFD life jackets emerged. Both were divers, Ken Ackroyd who was number one and George Hancock. Both were young men, peak fit and strong, picked for their ability to swim in difficult conditions. Their job would be to make a landing on the capsule and fix a lift wire from the ship's crane to haul it inboard. It was the safest way to rescue anyone who might be aboard. Safest that was, for the survivors. For the surface jumpers, the risks of getting caught in the roiling water between the capsule and the Star's hull, or of being swept away and lost or even simply of drowning, were high. It was a role that was given to the best of the best of the best and it carried a premium wage. Privately, Taff thought every time they went through this exercise, either as a drill or in a live rescue, that no amount of money was enough to pay these men for what they did.

Out loud he said, "All set, lads?"

"All set," said Ken. Ken Ackroyd was the more experienced of the two jumpers but even so he was only twenty seven or so. He had ten years offshore experience behind him, having started by splicing wire rope on a drilling rig in the early years of the Vietnamese oil boom and working his way up. In the hierarchy of the offshore diving service, in offshore terms, he was a veteran.

"They said it was a Smartie," he said.

Taff made no comment on the fact that they had clearly been listening in to the hailing channel. Nothing in a ship was private, least of all communication channels.

"That's so, lads," he said. "It's a bloody Whittaker. We all know they are unsteerable. Never mind, if we can come at the right angle, you can stay dry and work off the roof of the bugger."

Taff knew from the start that that was more realistic in theory than practice. The upper part of the curved shell of the Smartie was soaked with rain and spray, beaded with moisture. The suits that the two jumpers wore had built in rubber boots with deeply moulded soles. Under any normal circumstances they would grip on any surface, but a pitching capsule at sea, boarded from the heaving deck of a rescue vessel, were not normal circumstances. Both surface jumpers rigged themselves with a safety line, a slim nylon cord clipped to the suit harness and held at the other end to the deck rail. It was the last line of defence to save a man in the water.

On the starboard side, the Whittaker was transformed by

increasing proximity from a bright dot of colour against the dark water to a solid object as the distance closed. The beacon flashed regular bright strobe flashes, but even though the capsule seemed to be under some degree of control, every now and then a wave would lift the hull and expose the spinning prop in its circular guard.

"Engine's still running at least," said Ken.

Taff grunted. "Best mind the fucking prop, boyo," he said.

The propeller of the little capsule was shrouded in a stainless steel tunnel guide that swivelled to steer the capsule. In theory it also protected swimmers from injury by the spinning blades. Even so the tunnel shroud created vortex currents in the proximity of the prop that could draw in the unwary. It was a risk to be considered.

The Star edged ever closer, matching the capsule's erratic drift to bring it close to the rail-less section of the aft deck that was marked 'rescue zone' in huge yellow letters painted on the hull. Given the wind direction, as the two came close, the capsule would lie in the lee of the ship's hull, protected from the worst of the weather.

The best laid plans of mice and men, as the man said, often go awry. Tropical storms, whatever their intensity, are unpredictable beasts, full of erratic cross winds and random seas that come up out of the regular runs of wind and weather and they can trap even the most skilled and experienced helmsman.

Johnny Simpson, as a member of the marine crew, was to a degree separate from the salvage team. All of them were sailors, but the marine crew were involved only in the business of sailing the ship. They worked the standard watch system that the Royal Navy had evolved three centuries ago and drew a standard salary. Salvage crews worked twelve hours on and twelve off, and their pay, beyond a basic minimum, was based round the mighty bonuses based on the value of a wreck.

Marine crew were salaried on a different scale to salvage crew, but as a sort of rough compensation, they had no entitlement to the generous salvage bonuses.

There was, of course, cross over between the two groups. The most coveted positions on the Star were Marine crew sailors who, at need, switched roles when the ship was actually involved with a casualty, a system that provided the best of both worlds, even though the switching of roles resulted in gaps in the watch system that had to be covered by other sailors and that in itself cause a degree of resentment among the less favoured members of the crew.

Johnny Simpson was simply Marine crew, meaning that he was responsible for ship handling. As the Star's duty watch officer that night, he was just young enough to think of piloting the ship in a live rescue situation as a challenge, rather than a possibly lethal trap. He was thirty four that very day, and he thought it a fine birthday present after years of training and a good deal of time constantly acting as number two, to finally take control of the ship in a real rescue.

That combination of youth, enthusiasm and determination to press on in situations where more experienced hands might fear to tread has been the downfall of many a man at sea. Johnny's ship handling on that early post typhoon morning, was textbook. He swung well clear of the Smartie to the windward, bringing the capsule well into the ship's sheltered leeside before swinging closer, allowing the bulk of the Star's hull to drift towards the life-raft under the impulse of the wind and sea. It was a delicate balance, requiring him to judge and compensate for the semi-random action of the elements by gently easing the power to the thruster props that drove the Star sideways on.

Down on the aft deck, Ken Ackroyd, the duty surface jumper, was gauging his moment with immense care. His job would be to jump from the Star's deck onto the curved egg of the capsule's canopy, and fix the lifting eye from the swinging crane wire so that the whole thing could be hauled out of the water. He was waiting for that fleeting moment when the chance combination of wind and sea action would bring the capsule within range. It was essential that someone should be on the outside of the capsule's hull to fix the hauling/lifting line and, because of that, anticipating the need to board in hard conditions, the upperpart of the lifeboat's hull was clad in high friction material that resisted slippage no matter how wet it happened to be. As the waves heaved the Smartie up and down, Ken felt mentally for the rhythm that he knew was there. To make the jump properly demanded a near Zen-like state of concentration. He reached far down inside himself. And for those few seconds before the moment came for action, the wind and sea seemed suddenly somewhere far away, something that no longer concerned him. His concentration narrowed to a fine point of focus. No matter how random the rise and fall, Ken knew, well and sure, that the moment would come when the heave of the Star's deck would coincide with the capsule's rise allowing a soft-ish landing on the hull.

The yellow/orange flattened sphere of the Whittaker edged ever closer, slowing a little as the wind speed dropped in the lee of the Star's hull. Finally the moment came near. Ken tensed ready for the jump, watching the curved yellow egg ease up towards him out of the surface turmoil, before it fell away again on the swell. Like every jumper it was at such times he was at his most alive, every single nerve aware and in contact with the world. Colours were brighter, sounds sharper, drops of spume on the nearby deck winch stood out like spherical diamonds in the work lights.

Soon, he thought as the Smartie rose on the next crest. The little boat was very close now, close enough to read the faded transfer stuck to the hatch next to the release lever. It said: 'HATCH TO REMAIN CLOSED AT ALL TIMES WHEN AT SEA' in faded red letters against the yellow of the hull. The capsule rose slowly as if it were a lift in some gracious old building, easing inevitably towards the moment. The moment came. Ken uncoiled like a released spring, intending to clear the edge of the curved hull and land feet first on the non-slip pad on the roof, reaching at the same time for the stainless steel grab rail that ran around the curve of the hull in a silvery ring.

The crossing sea came at him as if, it too, had been waiting for that very moment. At the last second, the hull dropped away at the same time that the Star's canted deck twisted and rose in the other direction. What had been a five foot jump became twelve, and an increasing rapidly twelve at that. He landed awkwardly. What had been a limber leap turned clumsy. Suddenly he was sliding off the curved shell of the boat skidding past the spot where he had intended to grab the rails provided for just such an event. A cleat, jutting from the smooth curve of the hull, and intended as a mooring point, far from offering safe handhold, struck him on the left wing of his pelvis with the combined force of his leap and the merciless lift of the ocean. It was enough, even through the tough rubberised fabric of his dry suit, to break the bone and tear through a number of arteries in his groin. Most of the damage was painful but superficial, the partial severance of the femoral artery was not. Suddenly part of his anatomy that had been of no great interest to him, except when it was providing the most intense pleasure known to a man, became a focus of burning agony. Blood poured out of him like wine from an overturned jug. Within seconds the leggings of his immersion suit were slick and crimson.

The pain was so great, so intense and all consuming, that keeping position on the surface of the capsule was not important any longer. All that mattered in those last few seconds, was trying to raise his legs into a foetal crouch to reduce the agony in his crotch. It did not last long. The next wave threw him into the ocean like a rag doll, snapping the safety line tight and ripping the tether eye from his damaged suit. Even before George, his oppo, could take to the water to recover him, Ken, his floatation jacket ripped in the collision, and incapable of inflation, was gone. He sank, limp, into the depths without the effort of a final struggle to trouble his passing. In seconds, the violence of the surface was no more to him than a distant memory. A small patch of ocean was stained red for a few moments, then the water movement dispersed it.

Thirty feet deep, the storm was no more than a rumour from the world above and the water was kind and supportive like a downy feather bed. In the gentle embrace of the sea that had been his world, Ken crossed over to whatever lies beyond that final darkness.

Taff saw it all happen, saw his number one jumper miss his leap, smash like a fragile egg and then sink like a rock, and in that moment knew that he was beyond help. Taff was by nature, a gentle and caring man but he had been first hardened in combat, and then toughened in the salvage game. He knew better than to waste more lives in what must surely be a futile gesture, even if the alternative was heartbreaking.

He grabbed George's harness just in time, and hauled him bodily, and none too gently, away from the edge.

"No, lad," he yelled into George's ear against the screaming of the wind. "Fucking leave it. He's gone."

George seemed unable to comprehend that the great adventure had suddenly turned sour, and that a situation that had seemed under control had suddenly grown teeth and attacked them.

"But Taff," he shouted, "I can't leave him to drown. He's one of ours, for fuck's sake." Tears were already streaming against the wind but he didn't even know it.

Taff was shouting back over the wind, all the time hanging onto George's safety harness like grim death. "You can't bloody help him now," he said. "He's dead already. Enough of jumping the bloody thing, try to snag the lifting eye with a hook, boyo."

It was never intended to be a real solution. Taff intended no more than to occupy his panic-stricken subordinate, to give him something positive to do, anything to stop him attempting the impossible. Inside he was cold, shocked by losing a crewman, but like most men who work daily with mortal danger, Taff could turn off his emotional responses in the moment, at least for long enough to let him function in the event. Fear was for later, pain was for later, for the time being there was only the job, and the job had its own relentless priorities.

George took the boathook and looped the heavy lifting eye at the end of the pillar crane wire onto it. He flicked the wire free from its tether with a move that looked practised but was more or less pure luck. Right away the wire began to pull tight as the weight of the hook and the wire responded to the deck's rolling. From the end of the boathook the wire vanished upwards into the flying scud to the pulley at the tip of the crane jib far overhead. It was awkward and the hanging hook was heavy and hard to swing but George was pumped full of adrenaline. He took just one stabbing poke at the lifting eye of the capsule, shoved the crane hook well past it, and then, as it swung back with the movement of the ship he snagged the lifeboat as cleanly as an experienced fly fisherman gaffs a fish. The wire instantly pulled taut with the relative shift of the vessels and the capsule was half lifted out of the water as the Star pitched into the seas and the crane took the sudden strain. Up above, closeted in his tiny control cabin, Jacky Carson, the crane driver, would be cursing as he smoked the clutches on the drum of the wire cable, trying to ease the sudden strain. The boathook, caught between the crane hook and the lifting eye flicked up violently and flew out into the dark, tumbling end for end into the dim storm light

"Fucking hell," said Taff in an awed voice.

"Don't know if they do," said George, who was equally surprised by his success, "but I hear that they kiss In Heaven."

It was no more than the reflexive profanity of men at sea. A remark, made thousands of times before that moment, that would be repeated a million times more in the future, but it was enough, and just like that, the tension was broken.

Taff keyed his deck radio. He said, "Medic, medic to the aft deck please. Code red." Then into the radio again, he said, "Bridge. It's Taff. We have one crewman overboard. I repeat, one of my jumpers is overboard."

"Roger, Taff, we copy that, one over. Do you have eyes on him?"

"Negative bridge. We… we've lost him. As near as I can see, he was dead when he hit the water."

"Do you want to call a recovery pattern, Taff?"

That would mean the ship coming to a stop and steaming a fixed course, quartering and looking all the time for a tiny isolated scrap of bright orange against the ocean. In such conditions, given that Taff had seen with his own eyes that Ken had taken an injury that he could hardly have survived even in ideal conditions, he made his decision, keyed the mike and said, "Negative bridge. The man is dead for certain. No need to call a code."

"Copy that, Taff. No recovery pattern. Bridge is listening out."

Zac Rasmussen was on standby in the Star's hospital on C deck. He was sitting behind a steel desk in a comfy swivel chair that was the only bit of furniture in the place that was not fabricated from stainless steel. The tiny hospital was sterile and utilitarian. His heavy yellow immersion suit was unzipped and pooled round his waist, and the sleeves were tied in a rough knot in his lap. He was absently reading a paperback copy of Zorba the Greek to pass the waiting time. Looking down, he noticed that the left hand wrist seal of his suit was splitting. It hardly mattered on deck, but, should he end up in the water, that little nick would allow freezing liquid to creep in. Mentally, he made a note to swap out the suit at the ship's stores as soon as the emergency was done. For the moment it would do. Under the suit, he was wearing a tee shirt that advertised the delights of Caligula's club in Dubai over faded blue jeans. He was as prepared for action as it was possible to be, under the circumstances.

Beside each of the hospital bunks were the basic mechanics of disaster relief, a plastic pouch of straw coloured plasma expander, already fitted with a neatly coiled giving set nested against a space blanket that was part of a consignment someone at head office had clearly picked up cheap on the surplus market. The silvery plastic blankets were emblazoned in diagonal lines with the Mars Bar logo. Zac did not really approve of that kind of thing. Frivolity, he thought, was beneath the fundamental dignity of the occasion. Still, the foil blankets would work as well, no matter the silly advertising. The tannoy, set into the hospital ceiling tiles, bleeped abruptly, the 'heads up' signal for a message, and he swung his feet off the desk in anticipation. He was pulling the sleeves of the immersion suit on before the message came through.

"Medic," said the disembodied voice from the speaker. "Medic to the aft deck. We have recovered multiple survivors."

Zac zipped the suit's diagonal closure across his chest and started for the door. The emergency kit was right there beside it with all the intervention essentials inside. He clicked the hospital door latch reflexively on his way out. No one on the Star would steal anything, but there were controlled drugs on display on the ready use tray and old habits die very hard.

He clumped up the stairway to the aft deck access hatch, and it was only as he opened the door that he appreciated the violence of the storm for the first time. Waning she might be, past her extreme peak for certain, but the trailing edge of Typhoon Betsy still had plenty of energy behind it. The wind blasted straight into his face, threw the hood of his suit back in a misshapen balloon shape behind his head, and tried to snatch the chunky little medical bag out of his hand.

The Smartie was sitting on the open deck, resting on its lower hull. Out of the water it looked more like a nineteen fifties idea of a flying saucer than ever. The whole thing was vibrating slightly with the action of the wind and the stainless steel prop, in its steering tunnel, was turning slowly as the cooling water waste outlet still pumped weakly out of the exhaust onto the deck plates. To Zac, it looked like the last feeble pulse of a man dying of a massive bleed. Above the outlet, the access hatch was open and the interior showed as a weakly illuminated rectangle spilling a shaft of yellow light that picked up reflections from the driving drops of rain and wind-blown spume that crossed the deck in constant curtains.

Taff's deck crew had already laid a simple aluminium ladder way against the hatch. He climbed the ladder cautiously, moving rung by rung up the ladder, making sure of his handholds as he went.

CHAPTER TWENTY TWO

Chris Johanssen was Taff's number two that early post-typhoon morning, and to all obvious appearances, he was his normal self. The fact was though, that Chris was suffering a crisis of a sort that nothing from Zac's pharmacy could effectively help.

PTSD is not unusual among ex-servicemen, and certainly not unknown among offshore workers and it shows its ugly head either as mild insomnia and irritability, all the way through to full blown hallucinogenic episodes with flash backs, depression and recurrent nightmares.

It was Chris's bad luck that a salvage operation during an emergency is not supportive of emotional distress. He knew full well where the root of the dissatisfaction he felt with his of his life was rooted, but introspection was not enough to resolve the inner distress that he felt.

He was of an age – forty three, and old for a salvage-man – when a man looks back at the progress his life has made to date, and forwards toward whatever it might yet hold.

Sadly for Chris, looking back seemed to be a bleak vista all the way back to the dereliction of the valleys where he had been born.

He saw the ruined pits and the fallen headstocks as symptomatic of the fall of an old way of life and the destruction of an old culture that had left him bereft and adrift. Looking forwards, he felt profoundly that there was, or at least should be, more to his life. Chris was a man who felt constantly, and with a sort of deep ache, that he had far more to give than he had ever actualised.

Lack of fulfilment and diffuse unease is common enough. So common in fact that the concept of a midlife crisis has passed into popular cultures. The real problem was that offshore, at sea in a closed environment with periods of intense almost violent action interspersed with long periods of inactivity, with all too much time to think, are a perfect environment to foster depression.

No one on the Star had picked up on Chris's internal turmoil. Outwardly he seemed no different to his usual self. He went about his on board duties with exactly the same efficiency as always, organising rescue drills on a regular basis, servicing equipment, and standing his watches. In all respects he was himself, except one. At night, alone in his bunk, things were different. Every single time he fell asleep he found himself constantly carried along in his head by images of Africa, of dusty clearings of mud buildings and the smell of his own sweat and that of his patrol companions alongside him. The vision was too vivid too be called a dream. It was crystal clear and detailed right down to the whiff of the acrid aftershave that Jock 'Dusty' Miller always wore. The sun was too bright – too hot, even for West Africa. The dust hung in the air and he could even smell the gun oil from the Armalite he was carrying, a sharp scent, a mix of spent propellant and grease.

Each time he knew what was going to happen long before the first muzzle flashes of automatic fire from the cover of the hut started. The old gear that the guerrillas used, ancient variants of the AK47, allowed fire to lick in a flickering red and gold cloud around the muzzles every time they were fired. It gave an instant aiming point.

Then, inevitably, there was the answering fire, the sharp rattle of the Armalite and the tearing cloth ripple of an Ingram on full auto. Then it was done, there came the flash of the RPG and the collapse of the mud brick wall, and the sudden silence when even the wild birds were shocked into quiet.

The persistent flashbacks became, over a few weeks, an obsessive nightmare that crept into his waking hours. Again, because he was so good at what he did, Chris's problem went unnoticed. Besides, the culture that he lived in that required everyone to perform to the absolute maximum all the time, was not forgiving of a perceived weakness. It is the Catch 22 that has placed many a man on the mental rack of his own making. On the one hand being acutely aware of the problem, on the other being inwardly certain that he had no right to that emotional turmoil, that feeling those things at all was a weakness. It was in that conflicted state of mind, with only perhaps eighty percent of his mental abilities on the job, that Chris Johannsen stood on the deck beside the newly recovered Smartie and watched as Zac climbed the aluminium ladder to assess the casualties.

CHAPTER TWENTY THREE

With a mental squaring of the shoulders, Zac climbed the short ladder to the open hatch of the Whittaker. Beside the open hatch, standing on the narrow ledge that ran around the circumference of the capsule, Chris stood holding onto the chrome rail that ran round the hull.

The Smartie's weird shape was both a strength and a weakness. In the water the capsule could be tossed from wave to wave, could even, if the conditions produced such an effect, invert and float on its roof. None of those things could sink it, no matter how violent the movement was for the passengers inside. But all that stability was dependent on the support of the open ocean. On deck, resting on an unyielding hard surface, the stability characteristics of the Whittaker were another thing again. Even so, despite the uneasy shift of the capsule every time the ship rolled, Zac made it up the short ladder and through the hatch with no problems.

Inside the life capsule had the same foetid smell of salt water and terror that such vessels always have. Zac looked around him, mentally triaging the little party of survivors. Eight men, all in fair condition as far as he could tell, with the exception of an elderly Malay who seemed, by the way he supported his left arm with the right, to be suffering a fracture of the lower forearm. There were four women, three of them old and stout, one thin and hard-looking. There was also a Eurasian girl still with the bird-like build of slim Asiatic youth, and a child, a small girl who was all wide white eyes and pale skin in the semi-dark. Liwei's body was still slumped in the bilges. It did not need a close examination to see that he was past help. Zac left him where he lay, there were more vital concerns than respect for the dead.

Zac addressed the elderly man with the forearm injury.

"You first, uncle," he said. "You speak English?"

The old Malay looked, for a moment, as if he were faced with an abstract problem in higher mathematics, then he said, "Thank you, sir. Yes, I speak English very well." He said this in such a perfect accent that it might have suited an Oxbridge graduate.

Triage protocol ruled that, at this stage, the rescuers should clear the casualties en masse to a safe point below decks where a more formal triage could take place. Walking wounded first as they have the dual priority of needing most help and being most likely to respond well to treatment.

Zac said, "There is a ladder outside to access the deck. I need you to be aware that the slope is quite shallow so hold tight as far as you can. My colleague will help you down." He glanced around the cabin. "Does everybody understand?"

And so it went. The casualties left the capsule, for the most part moving as if with the tremulous uncertainty of extreme old age. The young girl, and the tough-looking Eurasian woman were last to go, and neither one could communicate beyond gestures. The woman came first and, outside the hatchway Chris positioned himself on the ledge that formed a rough landing platform outside the hatch and took her upper arm. He guided her gently onto the second rung of the ladder. Jenny finally had won her battle for survival.

Finally, there was the girl child. She was maybe eight years old, and in that first stage of hypovolemic shock that insulates the body from the mind, cutting off the pain and the fear at least temporarily. Chris took her arm to guide her to the ladder. She stood on the ledge of the Whittaker's hull, perhaps eight feet off the deck and fully exposed to the howling wind. As she reached tentatively out with her left foot, feeling for the top rung, a gust took her and very near hauled her out of Chris's grasp. For a moment, small and frail as she was, the sheer force of the wind was enough to take her like a living flag, strung out with the force of the blast. The jacket she was wearing was waterproof, slick with spray, and Chris could feel his grip slipping. Panic took him, as bitter and metallic tasting as a mouthful of fresh blood. Finally, inevitably, his grip failed and the small body was torn free.

She was less than five feet from the deck rail and her flight through the air was inelegant and tumbling but had just enough momentum to clear the scuppers and throw her over the rail. The sea accepted her body without even disturbing the roiling surface. One second she was there and the next... gone.

Witnessing this small tragedy, Chris Johanssen, ex-drug dealer, ex-legionnaire, ex-every bloody thing, suddenly felt the weight of mortal depression strike him in a way that it never done before, not even after that bungled job in the village. Blindly, not feeling the wind and rain anymore, he went down the ladder at a clumsy scramble, hampered by the weight of the immersion suit he wore. There was no real plan in his rush towards the deck side, just the need to do something – anything – to take back what had happened, to take the single wrong and set it right.

He was half way to the deck when the Star gave one of those rolls that were as violent as they were unpredictable. As the deck rolled, the capsule shifted its centre of gravity. Chris was caught in mid-climb, and he was thrown off the ladder and onto the deck. He was no sooner sprawled on the green painted deck plates, when the wave that had caused all these problems broke over the deck in a wall of foamy green. As it washed back overboard, the water washed him under the curve of the capsule's hull and wedged him neatly in the semi triangular space beside it.

Chris was no rookie. His life skills had been won in a thousand dangerous situations. His survival reflexes were strong and once the brief flash of memory had passed, he had time to think that the wave might well have done worse. He had a brief vision of himself smashed into the scuppers and through the freeing ports into the ocean or maybe shattered like an egg against any one of the dozens of bits of kit welded to the deck. His brief sense of comfort was short lived, before the whole situation became much worse. Even then he was in that strange state of awareness that accompanies violent action. Chris had time to appreciate every moment of it.

The first thing was a sense of pressure on his arm where it was trapped between the deck and the curve of the Whittaker's hull. It took brief seconds for him to realise that the capsule was rolling towards him. He had time for one short scream, time to wonder that such a sound was related to him, that that squeal of terror had really come from his throat. The capsule, out of the water, weighed a fraction less than three tonnes. That is not a massive load but it was enough. Like some later day victim of the iron virgin, Chris was crushed to a wedge of meat and bone between the capsule and the unyielding deck. It was good luck for him that the moving hull crushed his skull right at the start so that his passing was quick at least.

Zac, summoned from his improvised triage station by Chris's dying scream, was out and down the ladder, while the Smartie was still moving. He was too old a hand to think that there was any chance of his crewmate surviving such an injury. He had to shout to make himself heard over the wind. It was an odd way to pronounce death.

"Taff," he yelled, "he's gone for sure. Get me one of the bags from out of the store next to the hospital. And get a deckie with a bulk of timber to help me wedge this fucking Smartie before it kills half the fucking crew. Get the body bag first. Seeing this mess is not going to improve things for the survivors."

It was not the first time Taff had seen a death at sea but this instant reaction, this swapping the status of a crushed body from teammate and crewman to 'this mess' in a few words was still enough to shock him.

He said, "Is there nothing we could try?"

"You got any ideas?" said Zac. "Christ's sake, man, he looks like a hedgehog on a motorway. Now for fuck's sake, get that body bag before the next batch of survivors sees this mess."

"Well…" Taff looked at the spreading pool of gore around the body. It looked as if Chris's survival suit was no more than a balloon full of blood that was leaking all over. Where the blood reached the water on the deck there were little gory streaks trailing bright red threads against the clear pools. He said, "No, no, you're right, of course, boyo."

Zac, not a believer in soft treatment for bystanders, said, "I've people to treat here, man. There's no time to waste on those who are past help. Now let's get this done."

CHAPTER TWENTY FOUR

A nautical mile to the west, in a position that would have been well inside visibility range on a calm day, number four boat, the surviving Watercraft, alone in the churning ocean, had problems of its own. Sue Fangsu was tied up in a desperate attempt to stop the bleeding from four roughly amputated fingers with nothing more than the lifeboat's meagre first aid kit to help. Light years ago it seemed, she had done a basic first aid course, in the vague impression that it might lead to a nursing course and thence a way out of the sex trade. They had said that, to stop bleeding, it was almost always enough to cover the wound with sterile dressings and apply pressure. In the brightly lit training room where the only 'blood' was red dye it seemed so simple. This fine axiom was good for the usual range of open cuts from carving knife slips, or rips from broken glass, but the instructor had not envisioned four bleeding points that jetted small gory streams and poured onto the lifeboat's deck as if from a punctured hose. Try as Sue might to stem the flow, the bright red torrent refused her best efforts at control.

In every crowd there is a natural leader and, most often, there is also a natural rebel. Most of the survivors demonstrated this sad truth of Stockholm syndrome. In times of great stress, most people willingly transfer loyalty to whoever seems strong. If Sue Fangsu was willing to assume control of the injured crewman, most of the other passengers were ready to follow like sheep, gaping helplessly at the blood, in the fashion of road accident rubber neckers throughout the world. For his part, Harry, the cox was still fighting his small command through crossing seas that threatened his control constantly and he was willing enough to let her get on with it, there being nothing productive that he could offer in the way of help.

Then there was a natural rebel in that small terrified huddled group of survivors. Boat number four's natural rebel was a young engine room greaser called William Huan. He was only in the boat at all because of a highly developed sense of self-preservation that had allowed him to ignore protocol and save himself. Young master Hong had been at sea for eight months when the San Fong met her end. He was full of the certainty of youth, and the over confidence that results from small experience. William saw Harry as an old has-been, and when he took over as cox as a matter of course, reducing Huan's own status to that of a mere passenger, he resented it, and moreover he saw himself as the only seaman on the boat who could save the situation. Thus bolstered by illusion he was willing to cast himself as a natural leader, something which he was sadly not.

He looked at Sue's attempts at first aid with growing contempt. From his position opposite her in the narrow cabin, he had an excellent view of the soaked dressings and the spreading puddle of gore beside the glass fibre engine housing that was Sue's makeshift work space. He could also see all too clearly, the mutilated pad of flesh where a half hour before a human hand had been. He also had a better view than he would have wished of three severed fingers lying on the deck and that made him queasy, which, in turn, further fuelled his resentment.

He had the traditional Chinese male's contempt for low ranking women and felt Sue's moving in on what he saw as his own territory almost an affront to the natural order of things. No one in the rest of the little group of survivors seemed willing to take over so he simply crossed the narrow cabin, unstrapping his harness to allow him to move freely.

Harry, to give him his due, saw that the lad was not secured and he shouted a warning. The words were more or less lost to the wordless scream of the storm and the sea. The lifeboat was head to wind and the boat's movement was limited to a few feet of pitch. Even so, releasing the restraint harness that held William Huan in his seat was a silly thing to do. Under most conditions the most asinine foolishness goes unpunished by the Gods. This was not one of those occasions. The sea was moving in all directions at once and, even though the waves had diminished a little, the crossing sea that took the Watercraft on the port bow was more than she could handle. The bows rose with the sudden change of surface level, lifted maybe eight feet into the air and twisted violently to the right.

Watercraft are self-righting but for those people inside that glass fibre egg shell, safety in the event of a capsize depends on being strapped in place. Most of them were, and the tough nylon webbing held them to their seats as the little boat performed a move that did a fair impression of a washing machine drum on a fast spin. For those who were restrained, the result was a violent, stomach-churning shift of gravity from one direction to another and then, as the boat did as she was designed to do, and swung her centre of gravity back towards dead upright, the whole effect reversed itself.

There was a brief chorus of feminine squeals and masculine obscenities as the movement slowed. Sue and her patient were not secured of course. They fell free, not far, only a matter of five feet or so, and came to a bone jarring halt against the hull as it swapped floor for ceiling. Sue's descent was cushioned by the body of her patient and she landed squarely on the swell of his belly, contacting him shoulder first as it happened, and that at least protected her own vulnerable belly from the impact. She felt and heard something break. It seemed far away and, at first, she thought that one of her limbs was broken, but there was no pain, only that distant wet snapping sound like a twig broken forcefully underwater.

There was a brief shower of dirty water as the boat rolled over. It stank of the bilge, of wet rot and diesel, and it sloshed across her face so that her mouth was filled with the taste of it, salty and acrid. She spat and spat, trying to get rid of the awful clinging taste of it. Then the Watercraft began its return roll. The rattle of the old diesel, less than three inches from her right ear, was excruciatingly loud. It was designed to run with its salt water cooling interrupted for the few moments that a capsize takes but this boat was old, and had been old before the San Fong's owners had bought it surplus from a shipbreaker's yard in India.

As the self-righting took over the reverse roll, the chorus of horrified screams started again. The boat came to equilibrium and Sue Fangsu found herself lying against the soft cushion of her patient's body. His eyes were open. Wide open in fact and turned up in his head showing too much of the whites and his head was lying at a sick, acute angle against the deck plating.

Sue was no doctor but she knew enough to feel for a pulse. There was nothing of course, and William Huan, from opposite her, was venomous in his contempt, affecting what he saw as magnificent indifference in the face of death. In reality it was the first time he had ever seen a dead body and the sudden reality of it, the abrupt transition from life to its ending, unnerved him. Also there remained the need to assert his superiority over this child whore who had, as he saw it, usurped his position.

"Leave him be, woman," he said. "There's nothing you could do, so let him be."

Sue had been dominated and abused emotionally and physically by over confident young men all her life. Now all that dumb resentment welled up like a poison volcano from wellsprings inside her that she had barely realised existed.

Instead of regaining her seat, she turned to William where he sat. She was staggering a little with the lifeboat's shifts of orientation.

"You," she said. "You so fucking clever. You like steer the fucking boat, maybe? That takes real sailor not some fucking little boy. All fucking mouth like all of you, fucking arsehole." And she followed that, with her English exhausted, not adequate to her need to express her anger and contempt, with a stream of vile Cantonese.

Even then, that might have been the end of it, but William Huan was young and angry and more terrified by the capsize than he would have admitted, even to himself.

"Sit in your fucking seat, woman," he said. "You better stick to what you do best – lying on your fucking back, or maybe you better kneeling."

Sue Fangsu never knew where the knife came from. There are knives in every boat's emergency kit, so maybe it was one of those. It was a standard diver's deck knife, black plastic grip set with a blade eight inches long, thick and sturdy and saw-edged on the back of the blade. It was rusty and brown, speckled with disuse, but the edge was still keen Sheffield steel.

She simply stuck him, thrusting the blade at William, with no forethought. It was not intended as a killing stroke. It was no more than a gesture of contempt really, but the knife went in one side of his chest, and, skinny as he was, out the other. He looked down at the three inches or so of bloody steel, sticking out of his chest as if it had grown there. He shook his head in mute denial then opened his mouth as if to say something, but instead of words blood came instead. He collapsed to the lifeboat's floor. It was all very quick, the work of a second or two only.

Later, Harry, still giving all his concentration to steering the boat, would say that he never realised what had happened. Sue Fangsu looked back at him, as if the damage was nothing to do with her. The others looked on with wide eyes and shocked faces. They were still transfixed when a series of blasts on a ship's whistle announced the close arrival of the Typhoon Star.

CHAPTER TWENTY FIVE

In the hospital aboard the Star, Zac Rasmussen was working on the usual mixed casualties, who arrived in a steady stream from the upper deck. The hospital was a world apart from the rest of the ship at that stage in the rescue. In here, the overhead lighting, cold white fluorescents, was bright and merciless, throwing no shadows. The ports were all covered, the deadlights tightly screwed into place. At this stage of the rescue, triage on the upper deck was reduced to simply selecting living from dead. The dead were packaged into the long black plastic bags, zipped in to a darker night, and loaded into the now empty vegetable locker on C deck, reduced to anonymity. It was the best rough dignity that the Star's crew could offer.

Among the living casualties Sue Fangsu was causing Zac a problem. Shock, sometimes to the point of near catatonia, was not unknown among survivors, but Sue seemed completely unresponsive, even though she had very limited obvious physical injury. Zac's first thought was that there might be massive hidden internal damage, or maybe a head injury. He ran through the usual physical checks, pulse, respiration, blood pressure, feeling along her limbs for signs of fracture, checking her abdomen for the bruising or tension that would warn of crush damage.

It was all without result. He noted the slight bulge above her pubis that suggested early pregnancy, but 'obs and gynae' was well outside his field of expertise and he missed the signals that any country GP would have recognised instantly. As it was, after checking that the mild swelling was not obviously due to an internal increase in abdominal pressure that might be due to occult bleeding, he passed it off as slight overweight.

Sue's condition troubled him, the weakest point in any medic's armour is uncertainty. There was, he could see well enough, a degree of trauma there that went well beyond the natural shock of a survivor. That being said after a quick check, there was no time for anything more thorough. He marked Sue's record, a single sheet of xeroxed paper on a plastic clipboard, as being 'probably in shock' and left things at that.

As it happened, William Huan's body was the next 'patient' in. The bleeding, and there was a lot of it, had meant that the deck crew who had taken over on triage had directed William to the hospital rather than the morgue. Heavy bleeding cases are always checked by the medic in person, because in the later stages of exsanguination, blood pressure falls, and pulses idle to a near stop, so that it is quite possible for an inexperienced examiner to mistake near death for the real thing.

Zac ripped through William's boiler suit, slicing down the seams with a pair of strong backs, noting that the cloth was soaked below his neckline as far as his upper thighs. Generally it's possible to do a rough estimate of blood volume losses by checking how far down the body the blood stains had travelled. One thing Zac had not expected was the neat, almost surgical, incision just below the rib cage.

In training in A and E units on long ago Saturday nights, Zac had seen stab wounds before. He called over the deckhand who was helping out in the hospital that night.

"Do you see that wound, Steven?" he said to the guy, pointing to the mark on William's chest. "It's a stab wound, and that is a whole new problem. Not for him." He nodded at William's inert form. "This guy is long gone, but for us, it's a problem. No way did he do this to himself, so we need a witness to what I just found and that's you, okay? When we get back to the beach there is going to be all kinds of shit over this."

Sue Fangsu, who was seated on a green upholstered bench that stood against the bulkhead, suddenly spoke up. Hearing her voice, a message from the patient that they had thought was catatonic, was a shock.

"It was me," she said, and her voice had the inflection of a telephone robot reading off a number. "I kill him. He was shit. He try to make me small, to take away what I do. He like all his kind. He make me less than person, so I kill him."

Steven, a tall lugubrious-looking Geordie with a face like a sad beagle said, "Fucking hell, boss. Did she just say what I think she said?"

Zac, remembering a long ago, half day course on legal aspects of medical practice, said, "This woman has just made a voluntary confession to murder. You are a witness, Steven. You heard everything she said?"

"Sure but... look, mate, she's in shock. She don't know what she's saying. She's just survived a wreck. God knows what state she's in."

"Not our business to judge, Steven. Did you hear what she said? You heard her clearly. No chance of a mistake?"

"Yes, yes, I heard her."

"Right. We'll need to write down a statement for later. Best get it done as soon as we're done here. Also it would be best if we both say the same. Yes?"

"Sure. But what makes a kid like that do a thing like that? Christ's sake, boss, she's just a girl."

"Yes and that's not our business. Get that other one bagged up, will you? And don't bin what's left of his clothes. Keep everything as it is as much as possible. Mark the tag on his bag somehow. We don't want him mixed in with the other bodies. That one is a police case."

"How do we mark it?" asked Steven in a flat tone as if he was not able to assimilate the idea. "The tag, I mean?"

"There's two red magic markers on the desk over there. Put a couple of stripes on the label."

"Okay."

CHAPTER TWENTY SIX

Outside, on the aft deck, the weather was finally moderating, shifting down through a near gale, towards a strong breeze. The sea, that had so recently been a turmoil of violent crossing waters only a few hours before, was still rough, but it was gradually calming. The surface was a dull slate grey, and, scattered in a random pattern on the surface were the small dots of international rescue orange that marked where a lifejacket was still afloat.

This was the recovery phase of the rescue operation. Eight full hours after the ferry had finally gone to the bottom, there was no longer a realistic chance of improving on the numbers of survivors who were scattered through the accommodation below, gradually warming and realising that they were among the saved. From this point on, priorities would change. As long as the emphasis was on recovery, with a high chance of survivors, risks could be justified. From here on, the iron rule was not to risk the living to recover the dead.

Taff was still nominally supervising operations. It had been eight bruising hours and he was feeling the effects. It always ended this way in rescue jobs. There was at first the adrenaline rush of steaming at full speed towards the wreck site, then the near violent action of the recovery phase itself, when the sheer momentum of events carried him along. Now as the thrill of the immediate action drained way, there was always a flat almost depressive feeling that the crew could have done better.

All of the remaining orange dots in the ocean were, in theory, survivors, but Taff, old hand as he was, held no false hopes in that respect. Up on the bridge, the duty officer was steaming a square search pattern, dividing the grey surface into a neat series of squares that allowed them to check every single one of those bright orange targets. Just in case.

Looking out to starboard, Taff saw that the nearest of the lifejackets was not abandoned. As they closed on it he could see the man's head lolling in the water, holding in the air he could no longer breathe by the relentless mechanics of the RFD jacket he wore. Taff kneeled on the very edge of the deck watching him for the right moment, but he did not neglect the life line that clipped his own lifejacket to the deck rail – never risk the living for the dead.

The Star's iron flank slid gently through the water and the body gradually eased into range. As it came close, Taff hooked the tag on the floating lifejacket as deftly as a trout fisherman might gaff a fish. The body was, as he expected, a dead weight. He took the slack with a gentle jerk, holding the body against the Star's gentle wash and hauled the man inboard.

As the body lay on the deck, water seemed to pour from everywhere. Small salty freshets came from his mouth and nose draining back to the scuppers. Taff was no medic, but this was familiar territory and he knew enough to check this one.

Calling up the inner man who dealt with such things, while the real Taff, the man with human failings and emotions watched from a distance, Taff knelt beside the body, feeling the hardness of the deck plate against his knees, and deliberately ignored it, though increasingly, as the years took their toll, he found that little bit of isolation harder and harder to achieve. The man was certainly dead, though not so long dead as to lose the supple boneless fluidity of life.

Taff reached under the lifejacket. It was possibly the hardest thing of all to do. The touch was so intimate, in that moment it seemed almost indecent. It was too like the touch of a lover. Still protocol insisted that the recovery crew should check for identity documents. As it happened there was nothing.

Taff called across to the deck hand who was standing watching the recovery process in some horror.

"Joseph," he said, "get me a body bag, and then you better get another hand to help take him down to the locker. They'll tell you where to stow him."

Joseph the deck hand was young, maybe twenty at the most, and he was showing the dark shadows under his too wide eyes that the old timers called 'shock flesh'.

"Come on, lad," said Taff. "He's in no hurry, but I'm due for my relief."

Joseph jerked as if Taff had prodded him. "Should Zac not check him out?" he said.

"Boyo," said Taff not unkindly, "take a bit of advice from one who knows. We did what we could. Now, for this poor sod it wasn't enough to save him, but we can give him a bit of dignity. Now get the bag, will you?"

The deck hand left, leaving Taff kneeling beside the recently landed body. Quite spontaneously, speaking as naturally as if the dead man were a chance acquaintance at a cocktail party, Taff said, "I'm sorry, mate. It could easy enough have been me. Maybe sometime it will be. Whatever there is out there, you have a safe trip, mate."

The corpse, of course, said nothing.

CHAPTER TWENTY SEVEN

There are no real seasons in Singapore. The temperature is barely variable, clammy and hot all the year through, and the humidity is broken only by the rainy season. The Admiralty Court that administers all shipping with a Singapore registration, meets in an old colonialist building that has defied the efforts of various invaders to 'improve' it. During the brief Japanese reign of terror, it served as the headquarters for the Kempetai, the imperial Japanese version of the Gestapo. In happier times, the old court house even survived the modernising efforts of Lee Kwan Yu.

It stood alone during the destruction of the traditional red light quarter around Boogie Street, as the old bawdy houses fell around it. It stood, in solitary glory, through the relentless redevelopment of the old China town. Today it still stands, an enduring monument to the long gone imperialists who conceived it, with the deep carved stone Lion and Unicorn forever locked in dispute above the imposing, dark, hardwood mahogany framed and plate glass revolving door.

That morning, four months or so after Typhoon Betsy had become a matter of meteorological record, rather than a live storm centre, the Court of Enquiry into the loss of the inter-island ferry San Fong was reaching its conclusion, with the full trappings and majesty of the law.

The judge, Mr Justice Chang, senior justice in the Admiralty Court of chancery division of the Republic of Singapore, sat on a dais above the well of the courtroom in red robes, a horse hair wig, and an air of considerable splendour. Below him, the counsel for the various parties involved in the sinking sat behind their various desks. The dock, not required to contain an accused person in this civil court, acted instead as a convenient platform for the various witnesses to give their evidence.

As well as the formal area of the courtroom, tucked away at the back of the room like an after-thought, there were three long benches for the interested parties, and those witnesses who had already given their evidence. The benches were high backed and very upright, constructed in the fashion of a Victorian postural correction chair, or a chapel pew, and Zac Rasmussen and Taff Jennings were not comfortable as they observed proceedings. Zac was amusing himself by exchanging flirtatious glances with the pretty Chinese court reporter from the Singapore Times who was seated next to him. They had already given what testimony they could and now, two days into the inquest, the judge was preparing to deliver his verdict.

"It is the verdict of this investigation," he said, cadencing each word like a Church of England Bishop, "that the loss of the ferry San Fong was caused by the forces of nature and the sea. No blame can be laid on the master or his crew, and I find that the vessel was adequately maintained and well found. There is no suggestion that she was overloaded on that final voyage, and I find that there was ample provision of lifeboats and flotation aids for those aboard.

"Turning to the rescue operation carried out by the salvage vessel Typhoon Star, I find that the captain and crew behaved impeccably, and in full accordance with the laws of salvage and the custom and practice of the sea. No blame can be attached to the salvage team or their captain.

"I must now turn to the matter of the loss of life. This court finds that the two crewmen lost by the Typhoon Star died in pursuance of their duties and in an attempt to save survivors from the wreck. Accordingly I find that their deaths were by misadventure. As to the two hundred and eighty three souls who died in the floundering of the ferry, I find that their deaths were by accident.

"Turning now to the death of Mr William Huan within number four lifeboat, after the events that led to the sinking. For legal reasons this court is unable to pronounce on the cause and circumstances of that single fatality, and bows to the jurisdiction of the Singapore criminal court who I understand are preparing a case against a Miss Susan Fangsu. Because of that pending criminal case, I can say no more about that matter, and I defer the investigation into that single death to my learned brother in the Criminal Court.

"On the matter of salvage rights, clearly the San Fong is beyond all help in that respect, and I direct that the rights in possession of that wreck rest with the relevant insurers. As to the Watercraft lifeboat and the Whittaker escape capsule recovered from the sea, I direct that the salvage operators of the tug Typhoon Star are entitled to their full commercial value, estimated by the court as some eighty thousand dollars American. That is my award to the salvors in this case.

"That completes the court of inquiry into the loss of the ferry San Fong. Court now stands adjourned sine diem. Thank you, ladies and gentlemen, for your attention. I shall rise."

Four hours after that verdict, Zac and Taff were drinking in a sailor's bar. Years ago this place was an ancient knocking shop originally called the Palace of Earthly Delights. Later it was popular under various names with squaddies from the Singapore garrison. Now, in more straightened times, most of the military were long gone, but the naval base still provided just enough trade to keep things going.

Inside the bar was softly lit to the point of near semi-darkness.

Small lamps fixed to each table cast pools of yellow light and there was a strong smell of joss in the air that formed a blue fug with the smoke from the dozen or so joints that the clientele were smoking. Taff and Zac were not looking for any more exotic delights than a cool drink, and a few minutes of quiet.

"So," said Taff, "that's all she wrote. Another bloody wreck, another dollar."

"How many have you done?" asked Zac.

"Actual sinkings?" Taff thought for a moment. Finally he said, "Eleven, boyo, but this was the worst loss of life."

"Yes. That's always the hardest bit."

"Does it ever get to you, Zac? When they die? You must see more than most."

Zac looked almost surprised at the question. "No, Taff. Why would it? After all, they come to the finish, that's all. The price of life is, that, in the end, it finishes. We all of us owe the balance scales a death. The only thing is, to make the most of the journey."

"It seems so bloody pointless though," persisted Taff. "All those people. All those lives that they were living, and that woman who stabbed the guy in the lifeboat, she was just a girl really, and stressed to fuck, man. What will happen to her?"

"Singapore," said Zac judiciously, "still has a death penalty for murder."

"Christ."

"Not your business, man. We do what we do. We salvage ships, sometimes we save lives. We might think it would be nice to be God, but we aren't, and we never can be."

Taff took a pull at his drink, then said, "You believe in God, do you, Zac?"

"No."

"Just like that? No?"

"No, and yes – just like that. Look, Taff, if you feel so bad, why don't you buy yourself a few hours company from Madame Lu over there? She'll find you a pretty young one. Help you forget that fucking wreck. Besides in a few years' time, this will be just one of a hundred jobs that you did over the years."

Another ship, another sea, another storm, another group of sailors gathered in a warm dim space with the sea battering the plating a few feet from where they sat. A man spoke up out of the shadows.

"Does anyone remember that wreck?" Joseph said. "The San Fong?"

No one spoke, so he said, "I was a deckie learner then, on the old Typhoon Star. Anyhow it was one fuck of a storm, was that. Typhoon Betsy, they called it. I was just a kid, I remember being shit scared and listening to the lads talking, the way we are now. A long time ago, it seems now, a lot of water under the bridge since then. Anyhow this ferry, the San Fong, well they put out a pan pan call at maybe three in the morning. It was my first real emergency call, and I was so excited…"

And so the nightwatch continued, as the waves rushed and smashed against the hull, and the wind screamed its single idiot note, and the ship sailed on towards the new dawn.

There are no roses on a sailor's grave,
No lilies on an ocean wave.
The only tribute is the seagulls' sweeps,
And the teardrops that a sweetheart weeps.

Old German folk song adopted by World War Two U-boat crews and later by the British Merchant Navy, in a slightly different version. Usually quoted as the 'Merchant Navy hymn'.

NOTE FROM THE AUTHOR

This is not entirely a work of fiction. Most of the characters in Nightwatch are based on real people and real incidents, and the fact is that some readers are going to find some of their characters both unsympathetic and uncompromising.

Before you judge, remember that the pressure of salvage work at sea demands a mindset that most people will never have to develop. Most of those ready to pass the harshest judgements seem happy to do so from the safety of the land.

In particular the character of the medic, Zac Rasmussen, is based on a real life medic whose uncompromising attitude to the practice of off shore medicine is easily perceived as unsympathetic at best, and callous at worst.

In his defence, I can only say that I worked with the real 'Zac' in situations where a lesser man would have broken, and there was no one I would sooner choose to work with, and to do what was needed, without hesitation. That, in the final analysis, is truly the measure of the man. May the deep sea where he rests, give him more peace than he ever allowed himself in life.

As to the wreck of the ferry 'San Fong', the safety standards of the inter-island fleet in the largely unregulated regime in Indonesia, and the surrounding islands is well known. Old rust buckets still ply their trade and inevitably some of them still sink. The incidents in my fictionalised wreck all happened. The casualties were all real and in real life the dead stay dead.

JM 2019

Printed in Great Britain
by Amazon